GEORGE ELIOT NOVELLA COLLECTION

The Lifted Veil, Brother Jacob

GEORGE ELIOT

The Lifted Veil: Originally published in 1859, this work is in the public domain.

Brother Jacob: Originally published in 1864, this work is in the public domain.

No copyright claim is made with respect to public domain work.

This edition may reflect minor editorial revisions to the original text.

CONTENTS

THE LIFTED VEIL

Chapter 1	3
Chapter 2	29

BROTHER JACOB

Chapter 1	57
Chapter 2	72
Chapter 3	91

THE LIFTED VEIL

I

> Give me no light, great Heaven, but such as turns
> To energy of human fellowship;
> No powers beyond the growing heritage
> That makes completer manhood.

THE TIME of my end approaches. I have lately been subject to attacks of *angina pectoris*; and in the ordinary course of things, my physician tells me, I may fairly hope that my life will not be protracted many months. Unless, then, I am cursed with an exceptional physical constitution, as I am cursed with an exceptional mental character, I shall not much longer groan under the wearisome burthen of this earthly existence. If it were to be otherwise—if I were to live on to the age most men desire and provide for—I should for once have known whether the miseries of delusive expectation can outweigh the miseries of true provision. For

I foresee when I shall die, and everything that will happen in my last moments.

Just a month from this day, on September 20, 1850, I shall be sitting in this chair, in this study, at ten o'clock at night, longing to die, weary of incessant insight and foresight, without delusions and without hope. Just as I am watching a tongue of blue flame rising in the fire, and my lamp is burning low, the horrible contraction will begin at my chest. I shall only have time to reach the bell, and pull it violently, before the sense of suffocation will come. No one will answer my bell. I know why. My two servants are lovers, and will have quarrelled. My housekeeper will have rushed out of the house in a fury, two hours before, hoping that Perry will believe she has gone to drown herself. Perry is alarmed at last, and is gone out after her. The little scullery-maid is asleep on a bench: she never answers the bell; it does not wake her. The sense of suffocation increases: my lamp goes out with a horrible stench: I make a great effort, and snatch at the bell again. I long for life, and there is no help. I thirsted for the unknown: the thirst is gone. O God, let me stay with the known, and be weary of it: I am content. Agony of pain and suffocation—and all the while the earth, the fields, the pebbly brook at the bottom of the rookery, the fresh scent after the rain, the light of the morning through my chamber-window, the warmth of the hearth after the frosty air—will darkness close over them for ever?

Darkness—darkness—no pain—nothing but darkness: but I am passing on and on through the darkness: my thought stays in the darkness, but always with a sense of moving onward . . .

Before that time comes, I wish to use my last hours of ease and strength in telling the strange story of my experience. I have never fully unbosomed myself to any human being; I have never been encouraged to trust much in the sympathy of my fellow-men. But we have all a chance of meeting with some pity, some tenderness, some charity, when we are dead: it is the living only who cannot be forgiven—the living only from whom men's indulgence and reverence are held off, like the rain by the hard east wind. While the heart beats, bruise it—it is your only opportunity; while the eye can still turn towards you with moist, timid entreaty, freeze it with an icy unanswering gaze; while the ear, that delicate messenger to the inmost sanctuary of the soul, can still take in the tones of kindness, put it off with hard civility, or sneering compliment, or envious affectation of indifference; while the creative brain can still throb with the sense of injustice, with the yearning for brotherly recognition—make haste—oppress it with your ill-considered judgements, your trivial comparisons, your careless misrepresentations. The heart will by and by be still—"ubi saeva indignatio ulterius cor lacerare nequit"; the eye will cease to entreat; the ear will be deaf; the brain will have ceased from all wants as well as from all work. Then your charitable speeches may find vent; then you may remember and pity the toil and the struggle and the failure; then you may give due honour to the work achieved; then you may find extenuation for errors, and may consent to bury them.

That is a trivial schoolboy text; why do I dwell on it? It has little reference to me, for I shall leave no works behind me for men to honour. I have no near relatives who will make up, by weeping over my grave, for the wounds they inflicted on me when I was among them. It is only the story of my life that will perhaps win a little more sympathy from strangers when I am dead, than I ever believed it would obtain from my friends while I was living.

My childhood perhaps seems happier to me than it really was, by contrast with all the after-years. For then the curtain of the future was as impenetrable to me as to other children: I had all their delight in the present hour, their sweet indefinite hopes for the morrow; and I had a tender mother: even now, after the dreary lapse of long years, a slight trace of sensation accompanies the remembrance of her caress as she held me on her knee—her arms round my little body, her cheek pressed on mine. I had a complaint of the eyes that made me blind for a little while, and she kept me on her knee from morning till night. That unequalled love soon vanished out of my life, and even to my childish consciousness it was as if that life had become more chill I rode my little white pony with the groom by my side as before, but there were no loving eyes looking at me as I mounted, no glad arms opened to me when I came back. Perhaps I missed my mother's love more than most children of seven or eight would have done, to whom the other pleasures of life remained as before; for I was certainly a very sensitive child. I remember still the mingled trepidation and delicious excitement with which I was affected by the tramping of the horses on the pavement in the echoing stables, by the loud resonance of the groom's voices, by the booming bark of the dogs as my father's carriage thundered under the archway of the courtyard, by the din of the gong as it gave notice of luncheon and dinner. The measured tramp of soldiery which I sometimes heard—for my father's house lay near a county town where there were large barracks—made me sob and tremble; and yet when they were gone past, I longed for them to come back again.

I fancy my father thought me an odd child, and had little fondness for me; though he was very careful in fulfilling what he regarded as a parent's duties. But he was already past the middle of life, and I was not his only son. My mother had been his second wife, and he was five-and-forty when he married her. He was a firm, unbending, intensely orderly man, in root and stem a banker, but with a flourishing graft of the active landholder, aspiring to county influence: one of those people who are always like themselves from day to day, who are uninfluenced by the weather, and neither know melancholy nor high spirits. I held him in great awe, and appeared more timid and sensitive in his presence than at other times; a circumstance which, perhaps, helped to confirm him in the intention to educate me on a different plan from the prescriptive one with which he had complied in the case of my elder brother, already a tall youth at Eton. My brother was to be his representative and successor; he must go to Eton and Oxford, for the sake of making connexions, of course: my father was not a man to underrate the bearing of Latin satirists or Greek dramatists on the attainment of an aristocratic position. But, intrinsically, he had slight esteem for "those dead but sceptred spirits"; having qualified himself for forming an independent opinion by reading Potter's *Æschylus*, and dipping into Francis's *Horace*. To this negative view he added a positive one, derived from a recent connexion with mining speculations; namely, that a scientific education was the really useful training for a younger son. Moreover, it was clear that a shy, sensitive boy like me was not fit to encounter the rough experience of a public school. Mr. Letherall had said so very decidedly. Mr. Letherall was a large man in spectacles, who one day took my small head between his large hands, and pressed it here and there in an exploratory, auspicious manner—then placed each of his great thumbs on my temples, and pushed me a little way from him, and stared at me with glittering spectacles. The contemplation appeared to displease him, for he frowned sternly, and said to my father, drawing his thumbs across my eyebrows—

"The deficiency is there, sir—there; and here," he added, touching the upper sides of my head, "here is the excess. That must be brought out, sir, and this must be laid to sleep."

I was in a state of tremor, partly at the vague idea that I was the object of reprobation, partly in the agitation of my first hatred—hatred of this big, spectacled man, who pulled my head about as if he wanted to buy and cheapen it.

I am not aware how much Mr. Letherall had to do with the system afterwards adopted towards me, but it was presently clear that private tutors, natural history, science, and the modern languages, were the appliances by which the defects of my organization were to be remedied. I was very stupid about machines, so I was to be greatly occupied with them; I had no memory for classification, so it was particularly necessary that I should study systematic zoology and botany; I was hungry for human deeds and humane motions, so I was to be plentifully crammed with the mechanical powers, the elementary bodies, and the phenomena of electricity and magnetism. A better-constituted boy would certainly have profited under my intelligent tutors, with their scientific apparatus; and would, doubtless, have found the phenomena of electricity and magnetism as fascinating as I was, every Thursday, assured they were. As it was, I could have paired off, for ignorance of whatever was taught me, with the worst Latin scholar that was ever turned out of a classical academy. I read Plutarch, and Shakespeare, and Don Quixote by the sly, and supplied myself in that way with wandering thoughts, while my tutor was assuring me that "an improved man, as distinguished from an ignorant one, was a man who knew the reason why water ran downhill." I had no desire to be this improved man; I was glad of the running water; I could watch it and listen to it gurgling among the pebbles, and bathing the bright green water-plants, by the hour together. I did not want to know *why* it ran; I had perfect confidence that there were good reasons for what was so very beautiful.

There is no need to dwell on this part of my life. I have said enough to indicate that my nature was of the sensitive, unpractical order, and that it grew up in an uncongenial medium, which could never foster it into happy, healthy development. When I was sixteen I was sent to Geneva to complete my course of education; and the change was a very happy one to me, for the first sight of the Alps, with the setting sun on them, as we descended the Jura, seemed to me like an entrance into heaven; and the three years of my life there were spent in a perpetual sense of exaltation, as if from a draught of delicious wine, at the presence of Nature in all her awful loveliness.

You will think, perhaps, that I must have been a poet, from this early sensibility to Nature. But my lot was not so happy as that. A poet pours forth his song and *believes* in the listening ear and answering soul, to which his song will be floated sooner or later. But the poet's sensibility without his voice—the poet's sensibility that finds no vent but in silent tears on the sunny bank, when the noonday light sparkles on the water, or in an inward shudder at the sound of harsh human tones, the sight of a cold human eye—this dumb passion brings with it a fatal solitude of soul in the society of one's fellow-men. My least solitary moments were those in which I pushed off in my boat, at evening, towards the centre of the lake; it seemed to me that the sky, and the glowing mountain-tops, and the wide blue water, surrounded me with a cherishing love such as no human face had shed on me since my mother's love had vanished out of my life. I used to do as Jean Jacques did—lie down in my boat and let it glide where it would, while I looked up at the departing glow leaving one mountain-top after the other, as if the prophet's chariot of fire were passing over them on its way to the home of light. Then, when the white summits were all sad and corpse-like, I had to push homeward, for I was under careful surveillance, and was allowed no late wanderings. This disposition of mine was not favourable to the formation of intimate friendships among the numerous youths of my own age who are always to be found studying at Geneva. Yet I made *one* such friendship; and, singularly enough, it was with a youth whose intellectual tendencies were the very reverse of my own. I shall call him Charles Meunier; his real surname—an English one, for he was of English extraction—having since become celebrated. He was an orphan, who lived on a miserable pittance while he pursued the medical studies for which he had a special genius. Strange! that with my vague mind, susceptible and unobservant, hating inquiry and given up to contemplation, I should have been drawn towards a youth whose strongest passion was science. But the bond was not an intellectual one; it came from a source that can happily blend the stupid with the brilliant, the dreamy with the practical: it came from community of feeling. Charles was poor and ugly, derided by Genevese *gamins*, and not acceptable in drawing-rooms. I saw that he was isolated, as I was, though from a different cause, and, stimulated by a sympathetic resentment, I made timid advances towards him. It is enough to say that there sprang up as much comradeship between us as our different habits would allow; and in Charles's rare holidays we went up the Salève together, or took the boat to Vevay, while I listened dreamily to the monologues in which he unfolded his bold conceptions of future experiment and discovery. I mingled them confusedly in my thought with glimpses of blue water and delicate floating cloud, with the notes of birds and the distant glitter of the glacier. He knew quite well that my mind was half absent, yet he liked to talk to me in this way; for don't we talk of our hopes and our projects even to dogs and birds, when they love us? I have mentioned this one friendship because of its connexion with a strange and terrible scene which I shall have to narrate in my subsequent life.

This happier life at Geneva was put an end to by a severe illness, which is partly a blank to me, partly a time of dimly-remembered suffering, with the presence of my father by my bed from time to time. Then came the languid monotony of convalescence, the days gradually breaking into variety and distinctness as my strength enabled me to take longer and longer drives. On one of these more vividly remembered days, my father said to me, as he sat beside my sofa—

"When you are quite well enough to travel, Latimer, I shall take you home with me. The journey will amuse you and do you good, for I shall go through the Tyrol and Austria, and you will see many new places. Our neighbours, the Filmores, are come; Alfred will join us at Basle, and we shall all go together to Vienna, and back by Prague" . . .

My father was called away before he had finished his sentence, and he left my mind resting on the word *Prague*, with a strange sense that a new and wondrous scene was breaking upon me: a city under the broad sunshine, that seemed to me as if it were the summer sunshine of a long-past century arrested in its course—unrefreshed for ages by dews of night, or the rushing rain-cloud; scorching the dusty, weary, time-eaten grandeur of a people doomed to live on in the stale repetition of memories, like deposed and superannuated kings in their regal gold-inwoven tatters. The city looked so thirsty that the broad river seemed to me a sheet of metal; and the blackened statues, as I passed under their blank gaze, along the unending bridge, with their ancient garments and their saintly crowns, seemed to me the real inhabitants and owners of this place, while the busy, trivial men and women, hurrying to and fro, were a swarm of ephemeral visitants infesting it for a day. It is such grim, stony beings as these, I thought, who are the fathers of ancient faded children, in those tanned time-fretted dwellings that crowd the steep before me; who pay their court in the worn and crumbling pomp of the palace which stretches its monotonous length on the height; who worship wearily in the stifling air of the churches, urged by no fear or hope, but compelled by their doom to be ever old and undying, to live on in the rigidity of habit, as they live on in perpetual midday, without the repose of night or the new birth of morning.

A stunning clang of metal suddenly thrilled through me, and I became conscious of the objects in my room again: one of the fire-irons had fallen as Pierre opened the door to bring me my draught. My heart was palpitating violently, and I begged Pierre to leave my draught beside me; I would take it presently.

As soon as I was alone again, I began to ask myself whether I had been sleeping. Was this a dream—this wonderfully distinct vision—minute in its distinctness down to a patch of rainbow light on the pavement, transmitted through a coloured lamp in the shape of a star—of a strange city, quite unfamiliar to my imagination? I had seen no picture of Prague: it lay in my mind as a mere name, with vaguely-remembered historical associations—ill-defined memories of imperial grandeur and religious wars.

Nothing of this sort had ever occurred in my dreaming experience before, for I had often been humiliated because my dreams were only saved from being utterly disjointed and commonplace by the frequent terrors of nightmare. But I could not believe that I had been asleep, for I remembered distinctly the gradual breaking-in of the vision upon me, like the new images in a dissolving view, or the growing distinctness of the landscape as the sun lifts up the veil of the morning mist. And while I was conscious of this incipient vision, I was also conscious that Pierre came to tell my father Mr. Filmore was waiting for him, and that my father hurried out of the room. No, it was not a dream; was it—the thought was full of tremulous exultation—was it the poet's nature in me, hitherto only a troubled yearning sensibility, now manifesting itself suddenly as spontaneous creation? Surely it was in this way that Homer saw the plain of Troy, that Dante saw the abodes of the departed, that Milton saw the earthward flight of the Tempter. Was it that my illness had wrought some happy change in my organization—given a firmer tension to my nerves—carried off some dull obstruction? I had often read of such effects—in works of fiction at least. Nay; in genuine biographies I had read of the subtilizing or exalting influence of some diseases on the mental powers. Did not Novalis feel his inspiration intensified under the progress of consumption?

When my mind had dwelt for some time on this blissful idea, it seemed to me that I might perhaps test it by an exertion of my will. The vision had begun when my father was speaking of our going to

Prague. I did not for a moment believe it was really a representation of that city; I believed—I hoped it was a picture that my newly liberated genius had painted in fiery haste, with the colours snatched from lazy memory. Suppose I were to fix my mind on some other place—Venice, for example, which was far more familiar to my imagination than Prague: perhaps the same sort of result would follow. I concentrated my thoughts on Venice; I stimulated my imagination with poetic memories, and strove to feel myself present in Venice, as I had felt myself present in Prague. But in vain. I was only colouring the Canaletto engravings that hung in my old bedroom at home; the picture was a shifting one, my mind wandering uncertainly in search of more vivid images; I could see no accident of form or shadow without conscious labour after the necessary conditions. It was all prosaic effort, not rapt passivity, such as I had experienced half an hour before. I was discouraged; but I remembered that inspiration was fitful.

For several days I was in a state of excited expectation, watching for a recurrence of my new gift. I sent my thoughts ranging over my world of knowledge, in the hope that they would find some object which would send a reawakening vibration through my slumbering genius. But no; my world remained as dim as ever, and that flash of strange light refused to come again, though I watched for it with palpitating eagerness.

My father accompanied me every day in a drive, and a gradually lengthening walk as my powers of walking increased; and one evening he had agreed to come and fetch me at twelve the next day, that we might go together to select a musical box, and other purchases rigorously demanded of a rich Englishman visiting Geneva. He was one of the most punctual of men and bankers, and I was always nervously anxious to be quite ready for him at the appointed time. But, to my surprise, at a quarter past twelve he had not appeared. I felt all the impatience of a convalescent who has nothing particular to do, and who has just taken a tonic in the prospect of immediate exercise that would carry off the stimulus.

Unable to sit still and reserve my strength, I walked up and down the room, looking out on the current of the Rhone, just where it leaves the dark-blue lake; but thinking all the while of the possible causes that could detain my father.

Suddenly I was conscious that my father was in the room, but not alone: there were two persons with him. Strange! I had heard no footstep, I had not seen the door open; but I saw my father, and at his right hand our neighbour Mrs. Filmore, whom I remembered very well, though I had not seen her for five years. She was a commonplace middle-aged woman, in silk and cashmere; but the lady on the left of my father was not more than twenty, a tall, slim, willowy figure, with luxuriant blond hair, arranged in cunning braids and folds that looked almost too massive for the slight figure and the small-featured, thin-lipped face they crowned. But the face had not a girlish expression: the features were sharp, the pale grey eyes at once acute, restless, and sarcastic. They were fixed on me in half-smiling curiosity, and I felt a painful sensation as if a sharp wind were cutting me. The pale-green dress, and the green leaves that seemed to form a border about her pale blond hair, made me think of a Water-Nixie—for my mind was full of German lyrics, and this pale, fatal-eyed woman, with the green weeds, looked like a birth from some cold sedgy stream, the daughter of an aged river.

"Well, Latimer, you thought me long," my father said . . .

But while the last word was in my ears, the whole group vanished, and there was nothing between me and the Chinese printed folding-screen that stood before the door. I was cold and trembling; I could only totter forward and throw myself on the sofa. This strange new power had manifested itself again . . . But *was* it a power? Might it not rather be a disease—a sort of intermittent delirium, concentrating my energy of brain into moments of unhealthy activity, and leaving my saner hours all the more barren? I felt a dizzy sense of unreality in what my eye rested on; I grasped the bell convulsively, like one trying to free himself from nightmare, and rang it twice. Pierre came with a look of alarm in his face.

"Monsieur ne se trouve pas bien?" he said anxiously.

"I'm tired of waiting, Pierre," I said, as distinctly and emphatically as I could, like a man determined to be sober in spite of wine; "I'm afraid something has happened to my father—he's usually so punctual. Run to the Hôtel des Bergues and see if he is there."

Pierre left the room at once, with a soothing "Bien, Monsieur"; and I felt the better for this scene of simple, waking prose. Seeking to calm myself still further, I went into my bedroom, adjoining the *salon*, and opened a case of eau-de-Cologne; took out a bottle; went through the process of taking out the cork very neatly, and then rubbed the reviving spirit over my hands and forehead, and under my nostrils, drawing a new delight from the scent because I had procured it by slow details of labour, and by no strange sudden madness. Already I had begun to taste something of the horror that belongs to the lot of a human being whose nature is not adjusted to simple human conditions.

Still enjoying the scent, I returned to the salon, but it was not unoccupied, as it had been before I left it. In front of the Chinese folding-screen there was my father, with Mrs. Filmore on his right hand, and on his left—the slim, blond-haired girl, with the keen face and the keen eyes fixed on me in half-smiling curiosity.

"Well, Latimer, you thought me long," my father said . . .

I heard no more, felt no more, till I became conscious that I was lying with my head low on the sofa, Pierre, and my father by my side. As soon as I was thoroughly revived, my father left the room, and presently returned, saying—

"I've been to tell the ladies how you are, Latimer. They were waiting in the next room. We shall put off our shopping expedition to-day."

Presently he said, "That young lady is Bertha Grant, Mrs. Filmore's orphan niece. Filmore has adopted her, and she lives with them, so you will have her for a neighbour when we go home—perhaps for a near relation; for there is a tenderness between her and Alfred, I suspect, and I should be gratified by the match, since Filmore means to provide for her in every way as if she were his daughter. It had not occurred to me that you knew nothing about her living with the Filmores."

He made no further allusion to the fact of my having fainted at the moment of seeing her, and I would not for the world have told him the reason: I shrank from the idea of disclosing to any one what might be regarded as a pitiable peculiarity, most of all from betraying it to my father, who would have suspected my sanity ever after.

I do not mean to dwell with particularity on the details of my experience. I have described these two cases at length, because they had definite, clearly traceable results in my after-lot.

Shortly after this last occurrence—I think the very next day—I began to be aware of a phase in my abnormal sensibility, to which, from the languid and slight nature of my intercourse with others since my illness, I had not been alive before. This was the obtrusion on my mind of the mental process going forward in first one person, and then another, with whom I happened to be in contact: the vagrant, frivolous ideas and emotions of some uninteresting acquaintance—Mrs. Filmore, for example—would force themselves on my consciousness like an importunate, ill-played musical instrument, or the loud activity of an imprisoned insect. But this unpleasant sensibility was fitful, and left me moments of rest, when the souls of my companions were once more shut out from me, and I felt a relief such as silence brings to wearied nerves. I might have believed this importunate insight to be merely a diseased activity of the imagination, but that my prevision of incalculable words and actions proved it to have a fixed relation to the mental process in other minds. But this superadded consciousness, wearying and annoying enough when it urged on me the trivial experience of indifferent people, became an intense pain and grief when it seemed to be opening to me the souls of those who were in a close relation to me—when the rational talk, the graceful attentions, the wittily-turned phrases, and the kindly deeds, which used to make the web of their characters, were seen as if thrust asunder by a microscopic vision, that showed all the intermediate frivolities, all the suppressed egoism, all the struggling chaos of puerilities, meanness, vague capricious memories, and indolent make-shift thoughts, from which human words and deeds emerge like leaflets covering a fermenting heap.

At Basle we were joined by my brother Alfred, now a handsome, self-confident man of six-and-twenty—a thorough contrast to my fragile, nervous, ineffectual self. I believe I was held to have a sort of half-womanish, half-ghostly beauty; for the portrait-painters, who are thick as weeds at Geneva, had often asked me to sit to them, and I had been the model of a dying minstrel in a fancy picture. But I thoroughly disliked my own physique and nothing but the belief that it was a condition of poetic genius would have reconciled me to it. That brief hope was quite fled, and I saw in my face now nothing but the stamp of a morbid organization, framed for passive suffering —too feeble for the sublime resistance of poetic production. Alfred, from whom I had been almost constantly separated, and who, in his present stage of character and appearance, came before me as a perfect stranger, was bent on being extremely friendly and brother-like to me. He had the superficial kindness of a good-humoured, self-satisfied nature, that fears no rivalry, and has encountered no contrarieties. I am not sure that my disposition was good enough for me to have been quite free from envy towards him, even if our desires had not clashed, and if I had been in the healthy human condition which admits of generous confidence and charitable construction. There must always have been an antipathy between our natures. As it was, he became in a few weeks an object of intense hatred to me; and when he entered the room, still more when he spoke, it was as if a sensation of grating metal had set my teeth on edge. My diseased consciousness was more intensely and continually occupied with his thoughts and emotions, than with those of any other person who came in my way. I was perpetually exasperated with the petty promptings of his conceit and his love of patronage, with his self-complacent belief in Bertha Grant's passion for him, with his half-pitying contempt for me—seen not in the ordinary indications of intonation and phrase and slight action, which an acute and suspicious mind is on the watch for, but in all their naked skinless complication.

For we were rivals, and our desires clashed, though he was not aware of it. I have said nothing yet of the effect Bertha Grant produced in me on a nearer acquaintance. That effect was chiefly determined by the fact that she made the only exception, among all the human beings about me, to my unhappy gift of insight. About Bertha I was always in a state of uncertainty: I could watch the expression of her face, and speculate on its meaning; I could ask for her opinion with the real interest of ignorance; I could listen for her words and watch for her smile with hope and fear: she had for me the fascination of an unravelled destiny. I say it was this fact that chiefly determined the strong effect she produced on me: for, in the abstract, no womanly character could seem to have less affinity for that of a shrinking, romantic, passionate youth than Bertha's. She was keen, sarcastic, unimaginative, prematurely cynical, remaining critical and unmoved in the most impressive scenes, inclined to dissect all my favourite poems, and especially contemptous towards the German lyrics which were my pet literature at that time. To this moment I am unable to define my feeling towards her: it was not ordinary boyish admiration, for she was the very opposite, even to the colour of her hair, of the ideal woman who still remained to me the type of loveliness; and she was without that enthusiasm for the great and good, which, even at the moment of her strongest dominion over me, I should have declared to be the highest element of character. But there is no tyranny more complete than that which a self-centred negative nature exercises over a morbidly sensitive nature perpetually craving sympathy and support. The most independent people feel the effect of a man's silence in heightening their value for his opinion—feel an additional triumph in conquering the reverence of a critic habitually captious and satirical: no wonder, then, that an enthusiastic self-distrusting youth should watch and wait before the closed secret of a sarcastic woman's face, as if it were the shrine of the doubtfully benignant deity who ruled his destiny. For a young enthusiast is unable to imagine the total negation in another mind of the emotions which are stirring his own: they may be feeble, latent, inactive, he thinks, but they are there—they may be called forth; sometimes, in moments of happy hallucination, he believes they may be there in all the greater strength because he sees no outward sign of them. And this effect, as I have intimated, was heightened to its utmost intensity in me, because Bertha was the only being who remained for me in the mysterious seclusion of soul that renders such youthful delusion possible. Doubtless there was another sort of fascination at work—that subtle physical attraction which delights in cheating our psychological predictions, and in compelling the men who paint sylphs, to fall in love with some *bonne et brave femme*, heavy-heeled and freckled.

Bertha's behaviour towards me was such as to encourage all my illusions, to heighten my boyish passion, and make me more and more dependent on her smiles. Looking back with my present wretched knowledge, I conclude that her vanity and love of power were intensely gratified by the belief that I had fainted on first seeing her purely from the strong impression her person had produced on me. The most prosaic woman likes to believe herself the object of a violent, a poetic passion; and without a grain of romance in her, Bertha had that spirit of intrigue which gave piquancy to the idea that the brother of the man she meant to marry was dying with love and jealousy for her sake. That she meant to marry my brother, was what at that time I did not believe; for though he was assiduous in his attentions to her, and I knew well enough that both he and my father had made up their minds to this result, there was not yet an understood engagement—there had been no explicit declaration; and Bertha habitually, while she flirted with my brother, and accepted his homage in a way that implied to him a thorough recognition of its intention, made me believe, by the subtlest looks and phrases—feminine nothings which could never be quoted against her—that he was really the object of her secret ridicule; that she thought him, as I did, a coxcomb, whom she would have pleasure in disappointing. Me she openly petted in my brother's presence, as if I were too young and sickly ever to be thought of as a lover; and that was the view he took of me. But I believe she must inwardly have delighted in the tremors into which she threw me by the coaxing way in which she patted my curls, while she laughed at my quotations. Such caresses were always given in the presence of our friends; for when we were alone together, she affected a much greater distance towards me, and now and then took the opportunity, by words or slight actions, to stimulate my foolish timid hope that she really preferred me. And why should she not follow her inclination? I was not in so advantageous a position as my brother, but I had fortune, I was not a year younger than she was, and she was an heiress, who would soon be of age to decide for herself.

The fluctuations of hope and fear, confined to this one channel, made each day in her presence a delicious torment. There was one deliberate act of hers which especially helped to intoxicate me. When we were at Vienna her twentieth birthday occurred, and as she was very fond of ornaments, we all took the opportunity of the splendid jewellers' shops in that Teutonic Paris to purchase her a birthday present of jewellery. Mine, naturally, was the least expensive; it was an opal ring—the opal was my favourite stone, because it seems to blush and turn pale as if it had a soul. I told Bertha so when I gave it her, and said that it was an emblem of the poetic nature, changing with the changing light of heaven and of woman's eyes. In the evening she appeared elegantly dressed, and wearing conspicuously all the birthday presents except mine. I looked eagerly at her fingers, but saw no opal. I had no opportunity of noticing this to her during the evening; but the next day, when I found her seated near the window alone, after breakfast, I said, "You scorn to wear my poor opal. I should have remembered that you despised poetic natures, and should have given you coral, or turquoise, or some other opaque unresponsive stone." "Do I despise it?" she answered, taking hold of a delicate gold chain which she always wore round her neck and drawing out the end from her bosom with my ring hanging to it; "it hurts me a little, I can tell you," she said, with her usual dubious smile, "to wear it in that secret place; and since your poetical nature is so stupid as to prefer a more public position, I shall not endure the pain any longer."

She took off the ring from the chain and put it on her finger, smiling still, while the blood rushed to my cheeks, and I could not trust myself to say a word of entreaty that she would keep the ring where it was before.

I was completely fooled by this, and for two days shut myself up in my own room whenever Bertha was absent, that I might intoxicate myself afresh with the thought of this scene and all it implied.

I should mention that during these two months—which seemed a long life to me from the novelty and intensity of the pleasures and pains I underwent—my diseased anticipation in other people's consciousness continued to torment me; now it was my father, and now my brother, now Mrs. Filmore or her husband, and now our German courier, whose stream of thought rushed upon me like a ringing in the ears not to be got rid of, though it allowed my own impulses and ideas to continue their uninterrupted course. It was like a preternaturally heightened sense of hearing, making audible to one a roar of sound where others find perfect stillness. The weariness and disgust of this involuntary intrusion into other souls was counteracted only by my ignorance of Bertha, and my growing passion for her; a passion enormously stimulated, if not produced, by that ignorance. She was my oasis of mystery in the dreary desert of knowledge. I had never allowed my diseased condition to betray itself, or to drive me into any unusual speech or action, except once, when, in a moment of peculiar bitterness against my brother, I had forestalled some words which I knew he was going to utter—a clever observation, which he had prepared beforehand. He had occasionally a slightly affected hesitation in his speech, and when he paused an instant after the second word, my impatience and jealousy impelled me to continue the speech for him, as if it were something we had both learned by rote. He coloured and looked astonished, as well as annoyed; and the words had no sooner escaped my lips than I felt a shock of alarm lest such an anticipation of words—very far from being words of course, easy to divine—should have betrayed me as an exceptional being, a sort of quiet energumen, whom every one, Bertha above all, would shudder at and avoid. But I magnified, as usual, the impression any word or deed of mine could produce on others; for no one gave any sign of having noticed my interruption as more than a rudeness, to be forgiven me on the score of my feeble nervous condition.

While this superadded consciousness of the actual was almost constant with me, I had never had a recurrence of that distinct prevision which I have described in relation to my first interview with Bertha; and I was waiting with eager curiosity to know whether or not my vision of Prague would prove to have been an instance of the same kind. A few days after the incident of the opal ring, we were paying one of our frequent visits to the Lichtenberg Palace. I could never look at many pictures in succession; for pictures, when they are at all powerful, affect me so strongly that one or two exhaust all my capability of contemplation. This morning I had been looking at Giorgione's picture of the cruel-eyed woman, said to be a likeness of Lucrezia Borgia. I had stood long alone before it, fascinated by the terrible reality of that cunning, relentless face, till I felt a strange poisoned sensation, as if I had long been inhaling a fatal odour, and was just beginning to be conscious of its effects. Perhaps even then I should not have moved away, if the rest of the party had not returned to this room, and announced that they were going to the Belvedere Gallery to settle a bet which had arisen between my brother and Mr. Filmore about a portrait. I followed them dreamily, and was hardly alive to what occurred till they had all gone up to the gallery, leaving me below; for I refused to come within sight of another picture that day. I made my way to the Grand Terrace, since it was agreed that we should saunter in the gardens when the dispute had been decided. I had been sitting here a short space, vaguely conscious of trim gardens, with a city and green hills in the distance, when, wishing to avoid the proximity of the sentinel, I rose and walked down the broad stone steps, intending to seat myself farther on in the gardens. Just as I reached the gravel-walk, I felt an arm slipped within mine, and a light hand gently pressing my wrist. In the same instant a strange intoxicating numbness passed over me, like the continuance or climax of the sensation I was still feeling from the gaze of Lucrezia Borgia. The gardens, the summer sky, the consciousness of Bertha's arm being within mine, all vanished, and I seemed to be suddenly in darkness, out of which there gradually broke a dim firelight, and I felt myself sitting in my father's leather chair in the library at home. I knew the fireplace—the dogs for the wood-fire—the black marble chimney-piece with the white marble medallion of the dying Cleopatra in the centre. Intense and hopeless misery was pressing on my soul; the light became stronger, for Bertha was entering with a candle in her hand—Bertha, my wife—with cruel eyes, with green jewels and green leaves on her white ball-dress; every hateful thought within her present to me . . . "Madman, idiot! why don't you kill yourself, then?" It was a moment of hell. I saw into her pitiless soul—saw its barren worldliness, its scorching hate—and felt it clothe me round like an air I was obliged to breathe. She came with her candle and stood over me with a bitter smile of contempt; I saw the great emerald brooch on her bosom, a studded serpent with diamond eyes. I shuddered—I despised this woman with the barren soul and mean thoughts; but I felt helpless before her, as if she clutched my bleeding heart, and would clutch it till the last drop of life-blood ebbed away. She was my wife, and we hated each other. Gradually the hearth, the dim library, the candle-light disappeared—seemed to melt away into a background of light, the green serpent with the diamond eyes remaining a dark image on the retina. Then I had a sense of my eyelids quivering, and the living daylight broke in upon me; I saw gardens, and heard voices; I was seated on the steps of the Belvedere Terrace, and my friends were round me.

    The tumult of mind into which I was thrown by this hideous vision made me ill for several days, and prolonged our stay at Vienna. I shuddered with horror as the scene recurred to me; and it recurred constantly, with all its minutiæ, as if they had been burnt into my memory; and yet, such is the madness of the human heart under the influence of its immediate desires, I felt a wild hell-braving joy that Bertha was to be mine; for the fulfilment of my former prevision concerning her first appearance before me, left me little hope that this last hideous glimpse of the future was the mere diseased play of my own mind, and had no relation to external realities. One thing alone I looked towards as a possible means of casting doubt on my terrible conviction—the discovery that my vision of Prague had been false—and Prague was the next city on our route.

Meanwhile, I was no sooner in Bertha's society again than I was as completely under her sway as before. What if I saw into the heart of Bertha, the matured woman—Bertha, my wife? Bertha, the *girl*, was a fascinating secret to me still: I trembled under her touch; I felt the witchery of her presence; I yearned to be assured of her love. The fear of poison is feeble against the sense of thirst. Nay, I was just as jealous of my brother as before—just as much irritated by his small patronizing ways; for my pride, my diseased sensibility, were there as they had always been, and winced as inevitably under every offence as my eye winced from an intruding mote. The future, even when brought within the compass of feeling by a vision that made me shudder, had still no more than the force of an idea, compared with the force of present emotion—of my love for Bertha, of my dislike and jealousy towards my brother.

It is an old story, that men sell themselves to the tempter, and sign a bond with their blood, because it is only to take effect at a distant day; then rush on to snatch the cup their souls thirst after with an impulse not the less savage because there is a dark shadow beside them for evermore. There is no short cut, no patent tram-road, to wisdom: after all the centuries of invention, the soul's path lies through the thorny wilderness which must be still trodden in solitude, with bleeding feet, with sobs for help, as it was trodden by them of old time.

My mind speculated eagerly on the means by which I should become my brother's successful rival, for I was still too timid, in my ignorance of Bertha's actual feeling, to venture on any step that would urge from her an avowal of it. I thought I should gain confidence even for this, if my vision of Prague proved to have been veracious; and yet, the horror of that certitude! Behind the slim girl Bertha, whose words and looks I watched for, whose touch was bliss, there stood continually that Bertha with the fuller form, the harder eyes, the more rigid mouth—with the barren, selfish soul laid bare; no longer a fascinating secret, but a measured fact, urging itself perpetually on my unwilling sight. Are you unable to give me your sympathy—you who react this? Are you unable to imagine this double consciousness at work within me, flowing on like two parallel streams which never mingle their waters and blend into a common hue? Yet you must have known something of the presentiments that spring from an insight at war with passion; and my visions were only like presentiments intensified to horror. You have known the powerlessness of ideas before the might of impulse; and my visions, when once they had passed into memory, were mere ideas—pale shadows that beckoned in vain, while my hand was grasped by the living and the loved.

In after-days I thought with bitter regret that if I had foreseen something more or something different—if instead of that hideous vision which poisoned the passion it could not destroy, or if even along with it I could have had a foreshadowing of that moment when I looked on my brother's face for the last time, some softening influence would have been shed over my feeling towards him: pride and hatred would surely have been subdued into pity, and the record of those hidden sins would have been shortened. But this is one of the vain thoughts with which we men flatter ourselves. We try to believe that the egoism within us would have easily been melted, and that it was only the narrowness of our knowledge which hemmed in our generosity, our awe, our human piety, and hindered them from submerging our hard indifference to the sensations and emotions of our fellows. Our tenderness and self-renunciation seem strong when our egoism has had its day—when, after our mean striving for a triumph that is to be another's loss, the triumph comes suddenly, and we shudder at it, because it is held out by the chill hand of death.

Our arrival in Prague happened at night, and I was glad of this, for it seemed like a deferring of a terribly decisive moment, to be in the city for hours without seeing it. As we were not to remain long in Prague, but to go on speedily to Dresden, it was proposed that we should drive out the next morning and take a general view of the place, as well as visit some of its specially interesting spots, before the heat became oppressive—for we were in August, and the season was hot and dry. But it happened that the ladies were rather late at their morning toilet, and to my father's politely-repressed but perceptible annoyance, we were not in the carriage till the morning was far advanced. I thought with a sense of relief, as we entered the Jews' quarter, where we were to visit the old synagogue, that we should be kept in this flat, shut-up part of the city, until we should all be too tired and too warm to go farther, and so we should return without seeing more than the streets through which we had already passed. That would give me another day's suspense—suspense, the only form in which a fearful spirit knows the solace of hope. But, as I stood under the blackened, groined arches of that old synagogue, made dimly visible by the seven thin candles in the sacred lamp, while our Jewish cicerone reached down the Book of the Law, and read to us in its ancient tongue—I felt a shuddering impression that this strange building, with its shrunken lights, this surviving withered remnant of medieval Judaism, was of a piece with my vision. Those darkened dusty Christian saints, with their loftier arches and their larger candles, needed the consolatory scorn with which they might point to a more shrivelled death-in-life than their own.

As I expected, when we left the Jews' quarter the elders of our party wished to return to the hotel. But now, instead of rejoicing in this, as I had done beforehand, I felt a sudden overpowering impulse to go on at once to the bridge, and put an end to the suspense I had been wishing to protract. I declared, with unusual decision, that I would get out of the carriage and walk on alone; they might return without me. My father, thinking this merely a sample of my usual "poetic nonsense," objected that I should only do myself harm by walking in the heat; but when I persisted, he said angrily that I might follow my own absurd devices, but that Schmidt (our courier) must go with me. I assented to this, and set off with Schmidt towards the bridge. I had no sooner passed from under the archway of the grand old gate leading an to the bridge, than a trembling seized me, and I turned cold under the midday sun; yet I went on; I was in search of something—a small detail which I remembered with special intensity as part of my vision. There it was—the patch of rainbow light on the pavement transmitted through a lamp in the shape of a star.

2

Before the autumn was at an end, and while the brown leaves still stood thick on the beeches in our park, my brother and Bertha were engaged to each other, and it was understood that their marriage was to take place early in the next spring. In spite of the certainty I had felt from that moment on the bridge at Prague, that Bertha would one day be my wife, my constitutional timidity and distrust had continued to benumb me, and the words in which I had sometimes premeditated a confession of my love, had died away unuttered. The same conflict had gone on within me as before—the longing for an assurance of love from Bertha's lips, the dread lest a word of contempt and denial should fall upon me like a corrosive acid. What was the conviction of a distant necessity to me? I trembled under a present glance, I hungered after a present joy, I was clogged and chilled by a present fear. And so the days passed on: I witnessed Bertha's engagement and heard her marriage discussed as if I were under a conscious nightmare—knowing it was a dream that would vanish, but feeling stifled under the grasp of hard-clutching fingers.

When I was not in Bertha's presence—and I was with her very often, for she continued to treat me with a playful patronage that wakened no jealousy in my brother—I spent my time chiefly in wandering, in strolling, or taking long rides while the daylight lasted, and then shutting myself up with my unread books; for books had lost the power of chaining my attention. My self-consciousness was heightened to that pitch of intensity in which our own emotions take the form of a drama which urges itself imperatively on our contemplation, and we begin to weep, less under the sense of our suffering than at the thought of it. I felt a sort of pitying anguish over the pathos of my own lot: the lot of a being finely organized for pain, but with hardly any fibres that responded to pleasure—to whom the idea of future evil robbed the present of its joy, and for whom the idea of future good did not still the uneasiness of a present yearning or a present dread. I went dumbly through that stage of the poet's suffering, in which he feels the delicious pang of utterance, and makes an image of his sorrows.

I was left entirely without remonstrance concerning this dreamy wayward life: I knew my father's thought about me: "That lad will never be good for anything in life: he may waste his years in an insignificant way on the income that falls to him: I shall not trouble myself about a career for him."

One mild morning in the beginning of November, it happened that I was standing outside the portico patting lazy old Cæsar, a Newfoundland almost blind with age, the only dog that ever took any notice of me—for the very dogs shunned me, and fawned on the happier people about me—when the groom brought up my brother's horse which was to carry him to the hunt, and my brother himself appeared at the door, florid, broad-chested, and self-complacent, feeling what a good-natured fellow he was not to behave insolently to us all on the strength of his great advantages.

"Latimer, old boy," he said to me in a tone of compassionate cordiality, "what a pity it is you don't have a run with the hounds now and then! The finest thing in the world for low spirits!"

"Low spirits!" I thought bitterly, as he rode away; "that is the sort of phrase with which coarse, narrow natures like yours think to describe experience of which you can know no more than your horse knows. It is to such as you that the good of this world falls: ready dulness, healthy selfishness, good-tempered conceit—these are the keys to happiness."

The quick thought came, that my selfishness was even stronger than his—it was only a suffering selfishness instead of an enjoying one. But then, again, my exasperating insight into Alfred's self-complacent soul, his freedom from all the doubts and fears, the unsatisfied yearnings, the exquisite tortures of sensitiveness, that had made the web of my life, seemed to absolve me from all bonds towards him. This man needed no pity, no love; those fine influences would have been as little felt by him as the delicate white mist is felt by the rock it caresses. There was no evil in store for *him*: if he was not to marry Bertha, it would be because he had found a lot pleasanter to himself.

Mr. Filmore's house lay not more than half a mile beyond our own gates, and whenever I knew my brother was gone in another direction, I went there for the chance of finding Bertha at home. Later on in the day I walked thither. By a rare accident she was alone, and we walked out in the grounds together, for she seldom went on foot beyond the trimly-swept gravel-walks. I remember what a beautiful sylph she looked to me as the low November sun shone on her blond hair, and she tripped along teasing me with her usual light banter, to which I listened half fondly, half moodily; it was all the sign Bertha's mysterious inner self ever made to me. To-day perhaps, the moodiness predominated, for I had not yet shaken off the access of jealous hate which my brother had raised in me by his parting patronage. Suddenly I interrupted and startled her by saying, almost fiercely, "Bertha, how can you love Alfred?"

She looked at me with surprise for a moment, but soon her light smile came again, and she answered sarcastically, "Why do you suppose I love him?"

"How can you ask that, Bertha?"

"What! your wisdom thinks I must love the man I'm going to marry? The most unpleasant thing in the world. I should quarrel with him; I should be jealous of him; our *ménage* would be conducted in a very ill-bred manner. A little quiet contempt contributes greatly to the elegance of life."

"Bertha, that is not your real feeling. Why do you delight in trying to deceive me by inventing such cynical speeches?"

"I need never take the trouble of invention in order to deceive you, my small Tasso"—(that was the mocking name she usually gave me). "The easiest way to deceive a poet is to tell him the truth."

She was testing the validity of her epigram in a daring way, and for a moment the shadow of my vision—the Bertha whose soul was no secret to me—passed between me and the radiant girl, the playful sylph whose feelings were a fascinating mystery. I suppose I must have shuddered, or betrayed in some other way my momentary chill of horror.

"Tasso!" she said, seizing my wrist, and peeping round into my face, "are you really beginning to discern what a heartless girl I am? Why, you are not half the poet I thought you were; you are actually capable of believing the truth about me."

The shadow passed from between us, and was no longer the object nearest to me. The girl whose light fingers grasped me, whose elfish charming face looked into mine—who, I thought, was betraying an interest in my feelings that she would not have directly avowed,—this warm breathing presence again possessed my senses and imagination like a returning siren melody which had been overpowered for an instant by the roar of threatening waves. It was a moment as delicious to me as the waking up to a consciousness of youth after a dream of middle age. I forgot everything but my passion, and said with swimming eyes—

"Bertha, shall you love me when we are first married? I wouldn't mind if you really loved me only for a little while."

Her look of astonishment, as she loosed my hand and started away from me, recalled me to a sense of my strange, my criminal indiscretion.

"Forgive me," I said, hurriedly, as soon as I could speak again; "I did not know what I was saying."

"Ah, Tasso's mad fit has come on, I see," she answered quietly, for she had recovered herself sooner than I had. "Let him go home and keep his head cool. I must go in, for the sun is setting."

I left her—full of indignation against myself. I had let slip words which, if she reflected on them, might rouse in her a suspicion of my abnormal mental condition—a suspicion which of all things I dreaded. And besides that, I was ashamed of the apparent baseness I had committed in uttering them to my brother's betrothed wife. I wandered home slowly, entering our park through a private gate instead of by the lodges. As I approached the house, I saw a man dashing off at full speed from the stable-yard across the park. Had any accident happened at home? No; perhaps it was only one of my father's peremptory business errands that required this headlong haste.

Nevertheless I quickened my pace without any distinct motive, and was soon at the house. I will not dwell on the scene I found there. My brother was dead—had been pitched from his horse, and killed on the spot by a concussion of the brain.

I went up to the room where he lay, and where my father was seated beside him with a look of rigid despair. I had shunned my father more than any one since our return home, for the radical antipathy between our natures made my insight into his inner self a constant affliction to me. But now, as I went up to him, and stood beside him in sad silence, I felt the presence of a new element that blended us as we had never been blent before. My father had been one of the most successful men in the money-getting world: he had had no sentimental sufferings, no illness. The heaviest trouble that had befallen him was the death of his first wife. But he married my mother soon after; and I remember he seemed exactly the same, to my keen childish observation, the week after her death as before. But now, at last, a sorrow had come—the sorrow of old age, which suffers the more from the crushing of its pride and its hopes, in proportion as the pride and hope are narrow and prosaic. His son was to have been married soon—would probably have stood for the borough at the next election. That son's existence was the best motive that could be alleged for making new purchases of land every year to round off the estate. It is a dreary thing onto live on doing the same things year after year, without knowing why we do them. Perhaps the tragedy of disappointed youth and passion is less piteous than the tragedy of disappointed age and worldliness.

As I saw into the desolation of my father's heart, I felt a movement of deep pity towards him, which was the beginning of a new affection—an affection that grew and strengthened in spite of the strange bitterness with which he regarded me in the first month or two after my brother's death. If it had not been for the softening influence of my compassion for him—the first deep compassion I had ever felt—I should have been stung by the perception that my father transferred the inheritance of an eldest son to me with a mortified sense that fate had compelled him to the unwelcome course of caring for me as an important being. It was only in spite of himself that he began to think of me with anxious regard. There is hardly any neglected child for whom death has made vacant a more favoured place, who will not understand what I mean.

Gradually, however, my new deference to his wishes, the effect of that patience which was born of my pity for him, won upon his affection, and he began to please himself with the endeavour to make me fill any brother's place as fully as my feebler personality would admit. I saw that the prospect which by and by presented itself of my becoming Bertha's husband was welcome to him, and he even contemplated in my case what he had not intended in my brother's—that his son and daughter-in-law should make one household with him. My softened feelings towards my father made this the happiest time I had known since childhood;—these last months in which I retained the delicious illusion of loving Bertha, of longing and doubting and hoping that she might love me. She behaved with a certain new consciousness and distance towards me after my brother's death; and I too was under a double constraint—that of delicacy towards my brother's memory and of anxiety as to the impression my abrupt words had left on her mind. But the additional screen this mutual reserve erected between us only brought me more completely under her power: no matter how empty the adytum, so that the veil be thick enough. So absolute is our soul's need of something hidden and uncertain for the maintenance of that doubt and hope and effort which are the breath of its life, that if the whole future were laid bare to us beyond to-day, the interest of all mankind would be bent on the hours that lie between; we should pant after the uncertainties of our one morning and our one afternoon; we should rush fiercely to the Exchange for our last possibility of speculation, of success, of disappointment: we should have a glut of political prophets foretelling a crisis or a no-crisis within the only twenty-four hours left open to prophecy. Conceive the condition of the human mind if all propositions whatsoever were self-evident except one, which was to become self-evident at the close of a summer's day, but in the meantime might be the subject of question, of hypothesis, of debate. Art and philosophy, literature and science, would fasten like bees on that one proposition which had the honey of probability in it, and be the more eager because their enjoyment would end with sunset. Our impulses, our spiritual activities, no more adjust themselves to the idea of their future nullity, than the beating of our heart, or the irritability of our muscles.

Bertha, the slim, fair-haired girl, whose present thoughts and emotions were an enigma to me amidst the fatiguing obviousness of the other minds around me, was as absorbing to me as a single unknown to-day—as a single hypothetic proposition to remain problematic till sunset; and all the cramped, hemmed-in belief and disbelief, trust and distrust, of my nature, welled out in this one narrow channel.

And she made me believe that she loved me. Without ever quitting her tone of *badinage* and playful superiority, she intoxicated me with the sense that I was necessary to her, that she was never at ease, unless I was near her, submitting to her playful tyranny. It costs a woman so little effort to beset us in this way! A half-repressed word, a moment's unexpected silence, even an easy fit of petulance on our account, will serve us as *hashish* for a long while. Out of the subtlest web of scarcely perceptible signs, she set me weaving the fancy that she had always unconsciously loved me better than Alfred, but that, with the ignorant fluttered sensibility of a young girl, she had been imposed on by the charm that lay for her in the distinction of being admired and chosen by a man who made so brilliant a figure in the world as my brother. She satirized herself in a very graceful way for her vanity and ambition. What was it to me that I had the light of my wretched provision on the fact that now it was I who possessed at least all but the personal part of my brother's advantages? Our sweet illusions are half of them conscious illusions, like effects of colour that we know to be made up of tinsel, broken glass, and rags.

We were married eighteen months after Alfred's death, one cold, clear morning in April, when there came hail and sunshine both together; and Bertha, in her white silk and pale-green leaves, and the pale hues of her hair and face, looked like the spirit of the morning. My father was happier than he had thought of being again: my marriage, he felt sure, would complete the desirable modification of my character, and make me practical and worldly enough to take my place in society among sane men. For he delighted in Bertha's tact and acuteness, and felt sure she would be mistress of me, and make me what she chose: I was only twenty-one, and madly in love with her. Poor father! He kept that hope a little while after our first year of marriage, and it was not quite extinct when paralysis came and saved him from utter disappointment.

I shall hurry through the rest of my story, not dwelling so much as I have hitherto done on my inward experience. When people are well known to each other, they talk rather of what befalls them externally, leaving their feelings and sentiments to be inferred.

We lived in a round of visits for some time after our return home, giving splendid dinner-parties, and making a sensation in our neighbourhood by the new lustre of our equipage, for my father had reserved this display of his increased wealth for the period of his son's marriage; and we gave our acquaintances liberal opportunity for remarking that it was a pity I made so poor a figure as an heir and a bridegroom. The nervous fatigue of this existence, the insincerities and platitudes which I had to live through twice over— through my inner and outward sense—would have been maddening to me, if I had not had that sort of intoxicated callousness which came from the delights of a first passion. A bride and bridegroom, surrounded by all the appliances of wealth, hurried through the day by the whirl of society, filling their solitary moments with hastily-snatched caresses, are prepared for their future life together as the novice is prepared for the cloister—by experiencing its utmost contrast.

Through all these crowded excited months, Bertha's inward self remained shrouded from me, and I still read her thoughts only through the language of her lips and demeanour: I had still the human interest of wondering whether what I did and said pleased her, of longing to hear a word of affection, of giving a delicious exaggeration of meaning to her smile. But I was conscious of a growing difference in her manner towards me; sometimes strong enough to be called haughty coldness, cutting and chilling me as the hail had done that came across the sunshine on our marriage morning; sometimes only perceptible in the dexterous avoidance of a *tête-à-tête* walk or dinner to which I had been looking forward. I had been deeply pained by this—had even felt a sort of crushing of the heart, from the sense that my brief day of happiness was near its setting; but still I remained dependent on Bertha, eager for the last rays of a bliss that would soon be gone for ever, hoping and watching for some after-glow more beautiful from the impending night.

I remember—how should I not remember?—the time when that dependence and hope utterly left me, when the sadness I had felt in Bertha's growing estrangement became a joy that I looked back upon with longing as a man might look back on the last pains in a paralysed limb. It was just after the close of my father's last illness, which had necessarily withdrawn us from society and thrown us more on each other. It was the evening of father's death. On that evening the veil which had shrouded Bertha's soul from me—had made me find in her alone among my fellow-beings the blessed possibility of mystery, and doubt, and expectation—was first withdrawn. Perhaps it was the first day since the beginning of my passion for her, in which that passion was completely neutralized by the presence of an absorbing feeling of another kind. I had been watching by my father's deathbed: I had been witnessing the last fitful yearning glance his soul had cast back on the spent inheritance of life—the last faint consciousness of love he had gathered from the pressure of my hand. What are all our personal loves when we have been sharing in that supreme agony? In the first moments when we come away from the presence of death, every other relation to the living is merged, to our feeling, in the great relation of a common nature and a common destiny.

In that state of mind I joined Bertha in her private sitting-room. She was seated in a leaning posture on a settee, with her back towards the door; the great rich coils of her pale blond hair surmounting her small neck, visible above the back of the settee. I remember, as I closed the door behind me, a cold tremulousness seizing me, and a vague sense of being hated and lonely—vague and strong, like a presentiment. I know how I looked at that moment, for I saw myself in Bertha's thought as she lifted her cutting grey eyes, and looked at me: a miserable ghost-seer, surrounded by phantoms in the noonday, trembling under a breeze when the leaves were still, without appetite for the common objects of human desires, but pining after the moon-beams. We were front to front with each other, and judged each other. The terrible moment of complete illumination had come to me, and I saw that the darkness had hidden no landscape from me, but only a blank prosaic wall: from that evening forth, through the sickening years which followed, I saw all round the narrow room of this woman's soul—saw petty artifice and mere negation where I had delighted to believe in coy sensibilities and in wit at war with latent feeling—saw the light floating vanities of the girl defining themselves into the systematic coquetry, the scheming selfishness, of the woman—saw repulsion and antipathy harden into cruel hatred, giving pain only for the sake of wreaking itself.

For Bertha too, after her kind, felt the bitterness of disillusion. She had believed that my wild poet's passion for her would make me her slave; and that, being her slave, I should execute her will in all things. With the essential shallowness of a negative, unimaginative nature, she was unable to conceive the fact that sensibilities were anything else than weaknesses. She had thought my weaknesses would put me in her power, and she found them unmanageable forces. Our positions were reversed. Before marriage she had completely mastered my imagination, for she was a secret to me; and I created the unknown thought before which I trembled as if it were hers. But now that her soul was laid open to me, now that I was compelled to share the privacy of her motives, to follow all the petty devices that preceded her words and acts, she found herself powerless with me, except to produce in me the chill shudder of repulsion—powerless, because I could be acted on by no lever within her reach. I was dead to worldly ambitions, to social vanities, to all the incentives within the compass of her narrow imagination, and I lived under influences utterly invisible to her.

She was really pitiable to have such a husband, and so all the world thought. A graceful, brilliant woman, like Bertha, who smiled on morning callers, made a figure in ball-rooms, and was capable of that light repartee which, from such a woman, is accepted as wit, was secure of carrying off all sympathy from a husband who was sickly, abstracted, and, as some suspected, crack-brained. Even the servants in our house gave her the balance of their regard and pity. For there were no audible quarrels between us; our alienation, our repulsion from each other, lay within the silence of our own hearts; and if the mistress went out a great deal, and seemed to dislike the master's society, was it not natural, poor thing? The master was odd. I was kind and just to my dependants, but I excited in them a shrinking, half-contemptuous pity; for this class of men and women are but slightly determined in their estimate of others by general considerations, or even experience, of character. They judge of persons as they judge of coins, and value those who pass current at a high rate.

After a time I interfered so little with Bertha's habits that it might seem wonderful how her hatred towards me could grow so intense and active as it did. But she had begun to suspect, by some involuntary betrayal of mine, that there was an abnormal power of penetration in me—that fitfully, at least, I was strangely cognizant of her thoughts and intentions, and she began to be haunted by a terror of me, which alternated every now and then with defiance. She meditated continually how the incubus could be shaken off her life—how she could be freed from this hateful bond to a being whom she at once despised as an imbecile, and dreaded as an inquisitor. For a long while she lived in the hope that my evident wretchedness would drive me to the commission of suicide; but suicide was not in my nature. I was too completely swayed by the sense that I was in the grasp of unknown forces, to believe in my power of self-release. Towards my own destiny I had become entirely passive; for my one ardent desire had spent itself, and impulse no longer predominated over knowledge. For this reason I never thought of taking any steps towards a complete separation, which would have made our alienation evident to the world. Why should I rush for help to a new course, when I was only suffering from the consequences of a deed which had been the act of my intensest will? That would have been the logic of one who had desires to gratify, and I had no desires. But Bertha and I lived more and more aloof from each other. The rich find it easy to live married and apart.

That course of our life which I have indicated in a few sentences filled the space of years. So much misery—so slow and hideous a growth of hatred and sin, may be compressed into a sentence! And men judge of each other's lives through this summary medium. They epitomize the experience of their fellow-mortal, and pronounce judgment on him in neat syntax, and feel themselves wise and virtuous—conquerors over the temptations they define in well-selected predicates. Seven years of wretchedness glide glibly over the lips of the man who has never counted them out in moments of chill disappointment, of head and heart throbbings, of dread and vain wrestling, of remorse and despair. We learn *words* by rote, but not their meaning; *that* must be paid for with our life-blood, and printed in the subtle fibres of our nerves.

But I will hasten to finish my story. Brevity is justified at once to those who readily understand, and to those who will never understand.

Some years after my father's death, I was sitting by the dim firelight in my library one January evening—sitting in the leather chair that used to be my father's—when Bertha appeared at the door, with a candle in her hand, and advanced towards me. I knew the ball-dress she had on—the white ball-dress, with the green jewels, shone upon by the light of the wax candle which lit up the medallion of the dying Cleopatra on the mantelpiece. Why did she come to me before going out? I had not seen her in the library, which was my habitual place for months. Why did she stand before me with the candle in her hand, with her cruel contemptuous eyes fixed on me, and the glittering serpent, like a familiar demon, on her breast? For a moment I thought this fulfilment of my vision at Vienna marked some dreadful crisis in my fate, but I saw nothing in Bertha's mind, as she stood before me, except scorn for the look of overwhelming misery with which I sat before her . . . "Fool, idiot, why don't you kill yourself, then?"—that was her thought. But at length her thoughts reverted to her errand, and she spoke aloud. The apparently indifferent nature of the errand seemed to make a ridiculous anticlimax to my prevision and my agitation.

"I have had to hire a new maid. Fletcher is going to be married, and she wants me to ask you to let her husband have the public-house and farm at Molton. I wish him to have it. You must give the promise now, because Fletcher is going to-morrow morning—and quickly, because I'm in a hurry."

"Very well; you may promise her," I said, indifferently, and Bertha swept out of the library again.

I always shrank from the sight of a new person, and all the more when it was a person whose mental life was likely to weary my reluctant insight with worldly ignorant trivialities. But I shrank especially from the sight of this new maid, because her advent had been announced to me at a moment to which I could not cease to attach some fatality: I had a vague dread that I should find her mixed up with the dreary drama of my life—that some new sickening vision would reveal her to me as an evil genius. When at last I did unavoidably meet her, the vague dread was changed into definite disgust. She was a tall, wiry, dark-eyed woman, this Mrs. Archer, with a face handsome enough to give her coarse hard nature the odious finish of bold, self-confident coquetry. That was enough to make me avoid her, quite apart from the contemptuous feeling with which she contemplated me. I seldom saw her; but I perceived that she rapidly became a favourite with her mistress, and, after the lapse of eight or nine months, I began to be aware that there had arisen in Bertha's mind towards this woman a mingled feeling of fear and dependence, and that this feeling was associated with ill-defined images of candle-light scenes in her dressing-room, and the locking-up of something in Bertha's cabinet. My interviews with my wife had become so brief and so rarely solitary, that I had no opportunity of perceiving these images in her mind with more definiteness. The recollections of the past become contracted in the rapidity of thought till they sometimes bear hardly a more distinct resemblance to the external reality than the forms of an oriental alphabet to the objects that suggested them.

Besides, for the last year or more a modification had been going forward in my mental condition, and was growing more and more marked. My insight into the minds of those around me was becoming dimmer and more fitful, and the ideas that crowded my double consciousness became less and less dependent on any personal contact. All that was personal in me seemed to be suffering a gradual death, so that I was losing the organ through which the personal agitations and projects of others could affect me. But along with this relief from wearisome insight, there was a new development of what I concluded—as I have since found rightly—to be a provision of external scenes. It was as if the relation between me and my fellow-men was more and more deadened, and my relation to what we call the inanimate was quickened into new life. The more I lived apart from society, and in proportion as my wretchedness subsided from the violent throb of agonized passion into the dulness of habitual pain, the more frequent and vivid became such visions as that I had had of Prague—of strange cities, of sandy plains, of gigantic ruins, of midnight skies with strange bright constellations, of mountain-passes, of grassy nooks flecked with the afternoon sunshine through the boughs: I was in the midst of such scenes, and in all of them one presence seemed to weigh on me in all these mighty shapes—the presence of something unknown and pitiless. For continual suffering had annihilated religious faith within me: to the utterly miserable—the unloving and the unloved—there is no religion possible, no worship but a worship of devils. And beyond all these, and continually recurring, was the vision of my death—the pangs, the suffocation, the last struggle, when life would be grasped at in vain.

Things were in this state near the end of the seventh year. I had become entirely free from insight, from my abnormal cognizance of any other consciousness than my own, and instead of intruding involuntarily into the world of other minds, was living continually in my own solitary future. Bertha was aware that I was greatly changed. To my surprise she had of late seemed to seek opportunities of remaining in my society, and had cultivated that kind of distant yet familiar talk which is customary between a husband and wife who live in polite and irrevocable alienation. I bore this with languid submission, and without feeling enough interest in her motives to be roused into keen observation; yet I could not help perceiving something triumphant and excited in her carriage and the expression of her face—something too subtle to express itself in words or tones, but giving one the idea that she lived in a state of expectation or hopeful suspense. My chief feeling was satisfaction that her inner self was once more shut out from me; and I almost revelled for the moment in the absent melancholy that made me answer her at cross purposes, and betray utter ignorance of what she had been saying. I remember well the look and the smile with which she one day said, after a mistake of this kind on my part: "I used to think you were a clairvoyant, and that was the reason why you were so bitter against other clairvoyants, wanting to keep your monopoly; but I see now you have become rather duller than the rest of the world."

I said nothing in reply. It occurred to me that her recent obtrusion of herself upon me might have been prompted by the wish to test my power of detecting some of her secrets; but I let the thought drop again at once: her motives and her deeds had no interest for me, and whatever pleasures she might be seeking, I had no wish to baulk her. There was still pity in my soul for every living thing, and Bertha was living—was surrounded with possibilities of misery.

Just at this time there occurred an event which roused me somewhat from my inertia, and gave me an interest in the passing moment that I had thought impossible for me. It was a visit from Charles Meunier, who had written me word that he was coming to England for relaxation from too strenuous labour, and would like too see me. Meunier had now a European reputation; but his letter to me expressed that keen remembrance of an early regard, an early debt of sympathy, which is inseparable from nobility of character: and I too felt as if his presence would be to me like a transient resurrection into a happier pre-existence.

He came, and as far as possible, I renewed our old pleasure of making *tête-à-tête* excursions, though, instead of mountains and glacers and the wide blue lake, we had to content ourselves with mere slopes and ponds and artificial plantations. The years had changed us both, but with what different result! Meunier was now a brilliant figure in society, to whom elegant women pretended to listen, and whose acquaintance was boasted of by noblemen ambitious of brains. He repressed with the utmost delicacy all betrayal of the shock which I am sure he must have received from our meeting, or of a desire to penetrate into my condition and circumstances, and sought by the utmost exertion of his charming social powers to make our reunion agreeable. Bertha was much struck by the unexpected fascinations of a visitor whom she had expected to find presentable only on the score of his celebrity, and put forth all her coquetries and accomplishments. Apparently she succeeded in attracting his admiration, for his manner towards her was attentive and flattering. The effect of his presence on me was so benignant, especially in those renewals of our old *tête-à-tête* wanderings, when he poured forth to me wonderful narratives of his professional experience, that more than once, when his talk turned on the psychological relations of disease, the thought crossed my mind that, if his stay with me were long enough, I might possibly bring myself to tell this man the secrets of my lot. Might there not lie some remedy for me, too, in his science? Might there not at least lie some comprehension and sympathy ready for me in his large and susceptible mind? But the thought only flickered feebly now and then, and died out before it could become a wish. The horror I had of again breaking in on the privacy of another soul, made me, by an irrational instinct, draw the shroud of concealment more closely around my own, as we automatically perform the gesture we feel to be wanting in another.

When Meunier's visit was approaching its conclusion, there happened an event which caused some excitement in our household, owing to the surprisingly strong effect it appeared to produce on Bertha—on Bertha, the self-possessed, who usually seemed inaccessible to feminine agitations, and did even her hate in a self-restrained hygienic manner. This event was the sudden severe illness of her maid, Mrs. Archer. I have reserved to this moment the mention of a circumstance which had forced itself on my notice shortly before Meunier's arrival, namely, that there had been some quarrel between Bertha and this maid, apparently during a visit to a distant family, in which she had accompanied her mistress. I had overheard Archer speaking in a tone of bitter insolence, which I should have thought an adequate reason for immediate dismissal. No dismissal followed; on the contrary, Bertha seemed to be silently putting up with personal inconveniences from the exhibitions of this woman's temper. I was the more astonished to observe that her illness seemed a cause of strong solicitude to Bertha; that she was at the bedside night and day, and would allow no one else to officiate as head-nurse. It happened that our family doctor was out on a holiday, an accident which made Meunier's presence in the house doubly welcome, and he apparently entered into the case with an interest which seemed so much stronger than the ordinary professional feeling, that one day when he had fallen into a long fit of silence after visiting her, I said to him—

"Is this a very peculiar case of disease, Meunier?"

"No," he answered, "it is an attack of peritonitis, which will be fatal, but which does not differ physically from many other cases that have come under my observation. But I'll tell you what I have on my mind. I want to make an experiment on this woman, if you will give me permission. It can do her no harm—will give her no pain—for I shall not make it until life is extinct to all purposes of sensation. I want to try the effect of transfusing blood into her arteries after the heart has ceased to beat for some minutes. I have tried the experiment again and again with animals that have died of this disease, with astounding results, and I want to try it on a human subject. I have the small tubes necessary, in a case I have with me, and the rest of the apparatus could be prepared readily. I should use my own blood—take it from my own arm. This woman won't live through the night, I'm convinced, and I want you to promise me your assistance in making the experiment. I can't do without another hand, but it would perhaps not be well to call in a medical assistant from among your provincial doctors. A disagreeable foolish version of the thing might get abroad."

"Have you spoken to my wife on the subject?" I said, "because she appears to be peculiarly sensitive about this woman: she has been a favourite maid."

"To tell you the truth," said Meunier, "I don't want her to know about it. There are always insuperable difficulties with women in these matters, and the effect on the supposed dead body may be startling. You and I will sit up together, and be in readiness. When certain symptoms appear I shall take you in, and at the right moment we must manage to get every one else out of the room."

I need not give our farther conversation on the subject. He entered very fully into the details, and overcame my repulsion from them, by exciting in me a mingled awe and curiosity concerning the possible results of his experiment.

We prepared everything, and he instructed me in my part as

assistant. He had not told Bertha of his absolute conviction that Archer would not survive through the night, and endeavoured to persuade her to leave the patient and take a night's rest. But she was obstinate, suspecting the fact that death was at hand, and supposing that he wished merely to save her nerves. She refused to leave the sick-room. Meunier and I sat up together in the library, he making frequent visits to the sick-room, and returning with the information that the case was taking precisely the course he expected. Once he said to me, "Can you imagine any cause of ill-feeling this woman has against her mistress, who is so devoted to her?"

"I think there was some misunderstanding between them before her illness. Why do you ask?"

"Because I have observed for the last five or six hours—since, I fancy, she has lost all hope of recovery—there seems a strange prompting in her to say something which pain and failing strength forbid her to utter; and there is a look of hideous meaning in her eyes, which she turns continually towards her mistress. In this disease the mind often remains singularly clear to the last."

"I am not surprised at an indication of malevolent feeling in her," I said. "She is a woman who has always inspired me with distrust and dislike, but she managed to insinuate herself into her mistress's favour." He was silent after this, looking at the fire with an air of absorption, till he went upstairs again. He stayed away longer than usual, and on returning, said to me quietly, "Come now."

I followed him to the chamber where death was hovering. The dark hangings of the large bed made a background that gave a strong relief to Bertha's pale face as I entered. She started forward as she saw me enter, and then looked at Meunier with an expression of angry inquiry; but he lifted up his hand as it to impose silence, while he fixed his glance on the dying woman and felt her pulse. The face was pinched and ghastly, a cold perspiration was on the forehead, and the eyelids were lowered so as to conceal the large dark eyes. After a minute or two, Meunier walked round to the other side of the bed where Bertha stood, and with his usual air of gentle politeness towards her begged her to leave the patient under our care —everything should be done for her—she was no longer in a state to be conscious of an affectionate presence. Bertha was hesitating, apparently almost willing to believe his assurance and to comply. She looked round at the ghastly dying face, as if to read the confirmation of that assurance, when for a moment the lowered eyelids were raised again, and it seemed as if the eyes were looking towards Bertha, but blankly. A shudder passed through Bertha's frame, and she returned to her station near the pillow, tacitly implying that she would not leave the room.

The eyelids were lifted no more. Once I looked at Bertha as she watched the face of the dying one. She wore a rich *peignoir*, and her blond hair was half covered by a lace cap: in her attire she was, as always, an elegant woman, fit to figure in a picture of modern aristocratic life: but I asked myself how that face of hers could ever have seemed to me the face of a woman born of woman, with memories of childhood, capable of pain, needing to be fondled? The features at that moment seemed so preternaturally sharp, the eyes were so hard and eager—she looked like a cruel immortal, finding her spiritual feast in the agonies of a dying race. For across those hard features there came something like a flash when the last hour had been breathed out, and we all felt that the dark veil had completely fallen. What secret was there between Bertha and this woman? I turned my eyes from her with a horrible dread lest my insight should return, and I should be obliged to see what had been breeding about two unloving women's hearts. I felt that Bertha had been watching for the moment of death as the sealing of her secret: I thanked Heaven it could remain sealed for me.

Meunier said quietly, "She is gone." He then gave his arm to Bertha, and she submitted to be led out of the room.

I suppose it was at her order that two female attendants came into the room, and dismissed the younger one who had been present before. When they entered, Meunier had already opened the artery in the long thin neck that lay rigid on the pillow, and I dismissed them, ordering them to remain at a distance till we rang: the doctor, I said, had an operation to perform—he was not sure about the death. For the next twenty minutes I forgot everything but Meunier and the experiment in which he was so absorbed, that I think his senses would have been closed against all sounds or sights which had no relation to it. It was my task at first to keep up the artificial respiration in the body after the transfusion had been effected, but presently Meunier relieved me, and I could see the wondrous slow return of life; the breast began to heave, the inspirations became stronger, the eyelids quivered, and the soul seemed to have returned beneath them. The artificial respiration was withdrawn: still the breathing continued, and there was a movement of the lips.

Just then I heard the handle of the door moving: I suppose Bertha had heard from the women that they had been dismissed: probably a vague fear had arisen in her mind, for she entered with a look of alarm. She came to the foot of the bed and gave a stifled cry.

The dead woman's eyes were wide open, and met hers in full recognition—the recognition of hate. With a sudden strong effort, the hand that Bertha had thought for ever still was pointed towards her, and the haggard face moved. The gasping eager voice said—

"You mean to poison your husband . . . the poison is in the black cabinet . . . I got it for you . . . you laughed at me, and told lies about me behind my back, to make me disgusting . . . because you were jealous . . . are you sorry . . . now?"

The lips continued to murmur, but the sounds were no longer distinct. Soon there was no sound—only a slight movement: the flame had leaped out, and was being extinguished the faster. The wretched woman's heart-strings had been set to hatred and vengeance; the spirit of life had swept the chords for an instant, and was gone again for ever. Great God! Is this what it is to live again . . . to wake up with our unstilled thirst upon us, with our unuttered curses rising to our lips, with our muscles ready to act out their half-committed sins?

Bertha stood pale at the foot of the bed, quivering and helpless, despairing of devices, like a cunning animal whose hiding-places are surrounded by swift-advancing flame. Even Meunier looked paralysed; life for that moment ceased to be a scientific problem to him. As for me, this scene seemed of one texture with the rest of my existence: horror was my familiar, and this new revelation was only like an old pain recurring with new circumstances.

***

Since then Bertha and I have lived apart—she in her own neighbourhood, the mistress of half our wealth, I as a wanderer in foreign countries, until I came to this Devonshire nest to die. Bertha lives pitied and admired; for what had I against that charming woman, whom every one but myself could have been happy with? There had been no witness of the scene in the dying room except Meunier, and while Meunier lived his lips were sealed by a promise to me.

Once or twice, weary of wandering, I rested in a favourite spot, and my heart went out towards the men and women and children whose faces were becoming familiar to me; but I was driven away again in terror at the approach of my old insight—driven away to live continually with the one Unknown Presence revealed and yet hidden by the moving curtain of the earth and sky. Till at last disease took hold of me and forced me to rest here—forced me to live in dependence on my servants. And then the curse of insight—

of my double consciousness, came again, and has never left me. I know all their narrow thoughts, their feeble regard, their half-wearied pity.

***

It is the 20th of September, 1850. I know these figures I have just written, as if they were a long familiar inscription. I have seen them on this pace in my desk unnumbered times, when the scene of my dying struggle has opened upon me . . .

BROTHER JACOB

❦ I ❦

AMONG THE MANY fatalities attending the bloom of young desire, that of blindly taking to the confectionery line has not, perhaps, been sufficiently considered. How is the son of a British yeoman, who has been fed principally on salt pork and yeast dumplings, to know that there is satiety for the human stomach even in a paradise of glass jars full of sugared almonds and pink lozenges, and that the tedium of life can reach a pitch where plum-buns at discretion cease to offer the slightest excitement? Or how, at the tender age when a confectioner seems to him a very prince whom all the world must envy—who breakfasts on macaroons, dines on meringues, sups on twelfth-cake, and fills up the intermediate hours with sugar-candy or peppermint—how is he to foresee the day of sad wisdom, when he will discern that the confectioner's calling is not socially influential, or favourable to a soaring ambition? I have known a man who turned out to have a metaphysical genius, incautiously, in the period of youthful buoyancy, commence his career as a dancing-master; and you may imagine the use that was made of this initial mistake by opponents who felt themselves bound to warn the public against his doctrine of the Inconceivable. He could not give up his dancing-lessons, because he made his bread by them, and metaphysics would not have found him in so much as salt to his bread. It was really the same with Mr. David Faux and the confectionery business. His uncle, the butler at the great house close by Brigford, had made a pet of him in his early boyhood, and it was on a visit to this uncle that the confectioners' shops in that brilliant town had, on a single day, fired his tender imagination. He carried home the pleasing illusion that a confectioner must be at once the happiest and the foremost of men, since the things he made were not only the most beautiful to behold, but the very best eating, and such as the Lord Mayor must always order largely for his private recreation; so that when his father declared he must be put to a trade, David chose his line without a moment's hesitation; and, with a rashness inspired by a sweet tooth, wedded himself irrevocably to confectionery. Soon, however, the tooth lost its relish and fell into blank indifference; and all the while, his mind expanded, his ambition took new shapes, which could hardly be satisfied within the sphere his youthful ardour had chosen. But what was he to do? He was a young man of much mental activity, and, above all, gifted with a spirit of contrivance; but then, his faculties would not tell with great effect in any other medium than that of candied sugars, conserves, and pastry. Say what you will about the identity of the reasoning process in all branches of thought, or about the advantage of coming to subjects with a fresh mind, the adjustment of butter to flour, and of heat to pastry, is *not* the best preparation for the office of prime minister; besides, in the present imperfectly-organized state of society, there are social barriers. David could invent delightful things in the way of drop-cakes, and he had the widest views of the sugar department; but in other directions he certainly felt hampered by the want of knowledge and practical skill; and the world is so inconveniently constituted, that the vague consciousness of being a fine fellow is no guarantee of success in any line of business.

This difficulty pressed with some severity on Mr. David Faux, even before his apprenticeship was ended. His soul swelled with an impatient sense that he ought to become something very remarkable—that it was quite out of the question for him to put up with a narrow lot as other men did: he scorned the idea that he could accept an average. He was sure there was nothing average about him: even such a person as Mrs. Tibbits, the washer-woman, perceived it, and probably had a preference for his linen. At that particular period he was weighing out gingerbread nuts; but such an anomaly could not continue. No position could be suited to Mr. David Faux that was not in the highest degree easy to the flesh and flattering to the spirit. If he had fallen on the present times, and enjoyed the advantages of a Mechanic's Institute, he would certainly have taken to literature and have written reviews; but his education had not been liberal. He had read some novels from the adjoining circulating library, and had even bought the story of *Inkle and Yarico*, which had made him feel very sorry for poor Mr. Inkle; so that his ideas might not have been below a certain mark of the literary calling; but his spelling and diction were too unconventional.

When a man is not adequately appreciated or comfortably placed in his own country, his thoughts naturally turn towards foreign climes; and David's imagination circled round and round the utmost limits of his geographical knowledge, in search of a country where a young gentleman of pasty visage, lipless mouth, and stumpy hair, would be likely to be received with the hospitable enthusiasm which he had a right to expect. Having a general idea of America as a country where the population was chiefly black, it appeared to him the most propitious destination for an emigrant who, to begin with, had the broad and easily recognizable merit of whiteness; and this idea gradually took such strong possession of him that Satan seized the opportunity of suggesting to him that he might emigrate under easier circumstances, if he supplied himself with a little money from his master's till. But that evil spirit, whose understanding, I am convinced, has been much overrated, quite wasted his time on this occasion. David would certainly have liked well to have some of his master's money in his pocket, if he had been sure his master would have been the only man to suffer for it; but he was a cautious youth, and quite determined to run no risks on his own account. So he stayed out his apprenticeship, and committed no act of dishonesty that was at all likely to be discovered, reserving his plan of emigration for a future opportunity. And the circumstances under which he carried it out were in this wise. Having been at home a week or two partaking of the family beans, he had used his leisure in ascertaining a fact which was of considerable importance to him, namely, that his mother had a small sum in guineas painfully saved from her maiden perquisites, and kept in the corner of a drawer where her baby-linen had reposed for the last twenty years—ever since her son David had taken to his feet, with a slight promise of bow-legs which had not been altogether unfulfilled. Mr. Faux, senior, had told his son very frankly, that he must not look to being set up in business by *him*: with seven sons, and one of them a very healthy and well-developed idiot, who consumed a dumpling about eight inches in diameter every day, it was pretty well if they got a hundred apiece at his death. Under these circumstances, what was David to do? It was certainly hard that he should take his mother's money; but he saw no other ready means of getting any, and it was not to be expected that a young man of his merit should put up with inconveniences that could be avoided. Besides, it is not robbery to take property belonging to your mother: she doesn't prosecute you. And David was very well behaved to his mother; he comforted her by speaking highly of himself to her, and assuring her that he never fell into the vices he saw practised by other youths of his own age, and that he was particularly fond of honesty. If his mother would have given him her twenty guineas as a reward of this noble disposition, he really would not have stolen them from her, and it would have been more agreeable to his feelings. Nevertheless, to an active mind like David's, ingenuity is not without its pleasures: it was rather an interesting occupation to become stealthily acquainted with the wards of his mother's simple key (not in the least like Chubb's patent), and to get one that would do its work equally well; and also to arrange a little drama by which he would escape suspicion, and run no risk of forfeiting the prospective hundred at his father's death, which would be convenient in the improbable case of his *not* making a large fortune in the "Indies."

First, he spoke freely of his intention to start shortly for Liverpool and take ship for America; a resolution which cost his good mother some pain, for, after Jacob the idiot, there was not one of her sons to whom her heart clung more than to her youngest-born, David. Next, it appeared to him that Sunday afternoon, when everybody was gone to church except Jacob and the cowboy, was so singularly favourable an opportunity for sons who wanted to appropriate their mothers' guineas, that he half thought it must have been kindly intended by Providence for such purposes. Especially the third Sunday in Lent; because Jacob had been out on one of his occasional wanderings for the last two days; and David, being a timid young man, had a considerable dread and hatred of Jacob, as of a large personage who went about habitually with a pitchfork in his hand.

Nothing could be easier, then, than for David on this Sunday afternoon to decline going to church, on the ground that he was going to tea at Mr. Lunn's, whose pretty daughter Sally had been an early flame of his, and, when the church-goers were at a safe distance, to abstract the guineas from their wooden box and slip them into a small canvas bag—nothing easier than to call to the cowboy that he was going, and tell him to keep an eye on the house for fear of Sunday tramps. David thought it would be easy, too, to get to a small thicket and bury his bag in a hole he had already made and covered up under the roots of an old hollow ash, and he had, in fact, found the hole without a moment's difficulty, had uncovered it, and was about gently to drop the bag into it, when the sound of a large body rustling towards him with something like a bellow was such a surprise to David, who, as a gentleman gifted with much contrivance, was naturally only prepared for what he expected, that instead of dropping the bag gently he let it fall so as to make it untwist and vomit forth the shining guineas. In the same moment he looked up and saw his dear brother Jacob close upon him, holding the pitchfork so that the bright smooth prongs were a yard in advance of his own body, and about a foot off David's. (A learned friend, to whom I once narrated this history, observed that it was David's guilt which made these prongs formidable, and that the "mens nil conscia sibi" strips a pitchfork of all terrors. I thought this idea so valuable, that I obtained his leave to use it on condition of suppressing his name.) Nevertheless, David did not entirely lose his presence of mind; for in that case he would have sunk on the earth or started backward; whereas he kept his ground and smiled at Jacob, who nodded his head up and down, and said, "Hoich, Zavy!" in a painfully equivocal manner. David's heart was beating audibly, and if he had had any lips they would have been pale; but his mental activity, instead of being paralysed, was stimulated. While he was inwardly praying (he always prayed when he was much frightened) —"Oh, save me this once, and I'll never get into danger again!"—he was thrusting his hand into his pocket in search of a box of yellow lozenges, which he had brought with him from Brigford among other delicacies of the same portable kind, as a means of conciliating proud beauty, and more particularly the beauty of Miss Sarah Lunn. Not one of these delicacies had he ever offered to poor Jacob, for David was not a young man to waste his jujubes and barley-sugar in giving pleasure to people from whom he expected nothing. But an idiot with equivocal intentions and a pitchfork is as well worth flattering and cajoling as if he were Louis Napoleon. So David, with a promptitude equal to the occasion, drew out his box of yellow lozenges, lifted the lid, and performed a pantomime with his mouth and fingers, which was meant to imply that he was delighted to see his dear brother Jacob, and seized the opportunity of making him a small present, which he would find particularly agreeable to the taste. Jacob, you understand, was not an intense idiot, but within a certain limited range knew how to choose the good and reject the evil: he took one lozenge, by way of test, and sucked it as if he had been a philosopher; then, in as great an ecstacy at its new and complex savour as Caliban at the taste of Trinculo's wine, chuckled and stroked this suddenly beneficent brother, and held out his hand for more; for, except in fits of anger, Jacob was not ferocious or needlessly predatory. David's courage half returned, and he left off praying; pouring a dozen lozenges into Jacob's palm, and trying to look very fond of him. He congratulated himself that he had formed the plan of going to see Miss Sally Lunn this afternoon, and that, as a consequence, he had brought with him these propitiatory delicacies: he was certainly a lucky fellow; indeed, it was always likely Providence should be fonder of him than of other apprentices, and since he *was* to be interrupted, why, an idiot was preferable to any other sort of witness. For the first time in his life, David thought he saw the advantage of idiots.

As for Jacob, he had thrust his pitchfork into the ground, and had thrown himself down beside it, in thorough abandonment to the unprecedented pleasure of having five lozenges in his mouth at once, blinking meanwhile, and making inarticulate sounds of gustative content. He had not yet given any sign of noticing the guineas, but in seating himself he had laid his broad right hand on them, and unconsciously kept it in that position, absorbed in the sensations of his palate. If he could only be kept so occupied with the lozenges as not to see the guineas before David could manage to cover them! That was David's best hope of safety; for Jacob knew his mother's guineas; it had been part of their common experience as boys to be allowed to look at these handsome coins, and rattle them in their box on high days and holidays, and among all Jacob's narrow experiences as to money, this was likely to be the most memorable.

"Here, Jacob," said David, in an insinuating tone, handing the box to him, "I'll give 'em all to you. Run!—make haste!—else somebody'll come and take 'em."

David, not having studied the psychology of idiots, was not aware that they are not to be wrought upon by imaginative fears. Jacob took the box with his left hand, but saw no necessity for running away. Was ever a promising young man wishing to lay the foundation of his fortune by appropriating his mother's guineas obstructed by such a day-mare as this? But the moment must come when Jacob would move his right hand to draw off the lid of the tin box, and then David would sweep the guineas into the hole with the utmost address and swiftness, and immediately seat himself upon them. Ah, no! It's of no use to have foresight when you are dealing with an idiot: he is not to be calculated upon. Jacob's right hand was given to vague clutching and throwing; it suddenly clutched the guineas as if they had been so many pebbles, and was raised in an attitude which promised to scatter them like seed over a distant bramble, when, from some prompting or other—probably of an unwonted sensation—it paused, descended to Jacob's knee, and opened slowly under the inspection of Jacob's dull eyes. David began to pray again, but immediately desisted—another resource having occurred to him.

"Mother! zinnies!" exclaimed the innocent Jacob. Then, looking at David, he said, interrogatively, "Box?"

"Hush! hush!" said David, summoning all his ingenuity in this severe strait. "See, Jacob!" He took the tin box from his brother's hand, and emptied it of the lozenges, returning half of them to Jacob, but secretly keeping the rest in his own hand. Then he held out the empty box, and said, "Here's the box, Jacob! The box for the guineas!" gently sweeping them from Jacob's palm into the box.

This procedure was not objectionable to Jacob; on the contrary, the guineas clinked so pleasantly as they fell, that he wished for a repetition of the sound, and seizing the box, began to rattle it very gleefully. David, seizing the opportunity, deposited his reserve of lozenges in the ground and hastily swept some earth over them. "Look, Jacob!" he said, at last. Jacob paused from his clinking, and looked into the hole, while David began to scratch away the earth, as if in doubtful expectation. When the lozenges were laid bare, he took them out one by one, and gave them to Jacob. "Hush!" he said, in a loud whisper, "Tell nobody—all for Jacob—hush—sh—sh! Put guineas in the hole—they'll come out like this!" To make the lesson more complete, he took a guinea, and lowering it into the hole, said, "Put in *so*." Then, as he took the last lozenge out, he said, "Come out *so*," and put the lozenge into Jacob's hospitable mouth.

Jacob turned his head on one side, looked first at his brother and then at the hole, like a reflective monkey, and, finally, laid the box of guineas in the hole with much decision. David made haste to add every one of the stray coins, put on the lid, and covered it well with earth, saying in his meet coaxing tone—

"Take 'm out to-morrow, Jacob; all for Jacob! Hush—sh—sh!"

Jacob, to whom this once indifferent brother had all at once become a sort of sweet-tasted fetish, stroked David's best coat with his adhesive fingers, and then hugged him with an accompaniment of that mingled chuckling and gurgling by which he was accustomed to express the milder passions. But if he had chosen to bite a small morsel out of his beneficent brother's cheek, David would have been obliged to bear it.

And here I must pause, to point out to you the short-sightedness of human contrivance. This ingenious young man, Mr. David Faux, thought he had achieved a triumph of cunning when he had associated himself in his brother's rudimentary mind with the flavour of yellow lozenges. But he had yet to learn that it is a dreadful thing to make an idiot fond of you, when you yourself are not of an affectionate disposition: especially an idiot with a pitchfork—obviously a difficult friend to shake off by rough usage.

It may seem to you rather a blundering contrivance for a clever young man to bury the guineas. But, if everything had turned out as David had calculated, you would have seen that his plan was worthy of his talents. The guineas would have lain safely in the earth while the theft was discovered, and David, with the calm of conscious innocence, would have lingered at home, reluctant to say good-bye to his dear mother while she was in grief about her guineas; till at length, on the eve of his departure, he would have disinterred them in the strictest privacy, and carried them on his own person without inconvenience. But David, you perceive, had reckoned without his host, or, to speak more precisely, without his idiot brother—an item of so uncertain and fluctuating a character, that I doubt whether he would not have puzzled the astute heroes of M. de Balzac, whose foresight is so remarkably at home in the future.

It was clear to David now that he had only one alternative before him: he must either renounce the guineas, by quietly putting them back in his mother's drawer (a course not unattended with difficulty); or he must leave more than a suspicion behind him, by departing early the next morning without giving notice, and with the guineas in his pocket. For if he gave notice that he was going, his mother, he knew, would insist on fetching from her box of guineas the three she had always promised him as his share; indeed, in his original plan, he had counted on this as a means by which the theft would be discovered under circumstances that would themselves speak for his innocence; but now, as I need hardly explain, that well-combined plan was completely frustrated. Even if David could have bribed Jacob with perpetual lozenges, an idiot's secrecy is itself betrayal. He dared not even go to tea at Mr. Lunn's, for in that case he would have lost sight of Jacob, who, in his impatience for the crop of lozenges, might scratch up the box again while he was absent, and carry it home—depriving him at once of reputation and guineas. No! he must think of nothing all the rest of this day, but of coaxing Jacob and keeping him out of mischief. It was a fatiguing and anxious evening to David; nevertheless, he dared not go to sleep without tying a piece of string to his thumb and great toe, to secure his frequent waking; for he meant to be up with the first peep of dawn, and be far out of reach before breakfast-time. His father, he thought, would certainly cut him off with a shilling; but what then? Such a striking young man as he would be sure to be well received in the West Indies: in foreign countries there are always openings—even for cats. It was probable that some Princess Yarico would want him to marry her, and make him presents of very large jewels beforehand; after which, he needn't marry her unless he liked. David had made up his mind not to steal any more, even from people who were fond of him: it was an unpleasant way of making your fortune in a world where you were likely to surprised in the act by brothers. Such alarms did not agree with David's constitution, and he had felt so much nausea this evening that no doubt his liver was affected. Besides, he would have been greatly hurt not to be thought well of in the world: he always meant to make a figure, and be thought worthy of the best seats and the best morsels.

    Ruminating to this effect on the brilliant future in reserve for him, David by the help of his check-string kept himself on the alert to seize the time of earliest dawn for his rising and departure. His brothers, of course, were early risers, but he should anticipate them by at least an hour and a half, and the little room which he had to himself as only an occasional visitor, had its window over the horse-block, so that he could slip out through the window without the least difficulty. Jacob, the horrible Jacob, had an awkward trick of getting up before everybody else, to stem his hunger by emptying the milk-bowl that was "duly set" for him; but of late he had taken to sleeping in the hay-loft, and if he came into the house, it would be on the opposite side to that from which David was making his exit. There was no need to think of Jacob; yet David was liberal enough to bestow a curse on him—it was the only thing he ever did bestow gratuitously. His small bundle of clothes was ready packed, and he was soon treading lightly on the steps of the horse-block, soon walking at a smart pace across the fields towards the thicket. It would take him no more than two minutes to get out the box; he could make out the tree it was under by the pale strip where the bark was off, although the dawning light was rather dimmer in the thicket. But what, in the name of—burnt pastry—was that large body with a staff planted beside it, close at the foot of the ash-tree? David paused, not to make up his mind as to the nature of the apparition—he had not the happiness of doubting for a moment that the staff was Jacob's pitchfork—but to gather the self-command necessary for addressing his brother with a sufficiently honeyed accent. Jacob was absorbed in scratching up the earth, and had not heard David's approach.

"I say, Jacob," said David in a loud whisper, just as the tin box was lifted out of the hole.

Jacob looked up, and discerning his sweet-flavoured brother, nodded and grinned in the dim light in a way that made him seem to David like a triumphant demon. If he had been of an impetuous disposition, he would have snatched the pitchfork from the ground and impaled this fraternal demon. But David was by no means impetuous; he was a young man greatly given to calculate consequences, a habit which has been held to be the foundation of virtue. But somehow it had not precisely that effect in David: he calculated whether an action would harm himself, or whether it would only harm other people. In the former case he was very timid about satisfying his immediate desires, but in the latter he would risk the result with much courage.

"Give it me, Jacob," he said, stooping down and patting his brother. "Let us see."

Jacob, finding the lid rather tight, gave the box to his brother in perfect faith. David raised the lids and shook his head, while Jacob put his finger in and took out a guinea to taste whether the metamorphosis into lozenges was complete and satisfactory.

"No, Jacob; too soon, too soon," said David, when the guinea had been tasted. "Give it me; we'll go and bury it somewhere else; we'll put it in yonder," he added, pointing vaguely toward the distance.

David screwed on the lid, while Jacob, looking grave, rose and grasped his pitchfork. Then, seeing David's bundle, he snatched it, like a too officious Newfoundland, stuck his pitchfork into it and carried it over his shoulder in triumph as he accompanied David and the box out of the thicket.

What on earth was David to do? It would have been easy to frown at Jacob, and kick him, and order him to get away; but David dared as soon have kicked the bull. Jacob was quiet as long as he was treated indulgently; but on the slightest show of anger, he became unmanageable, and was liable to fits of fury which would have made him formidable even without his pitchfork. There was no mastery to be obtained over him except by kindness or guile. David tried guile.

"Go, Jacob," he said, when they were out of the thicket—pointing towards the house as he spoke; "go and fetch me a spade—a spade. But give *me* the bundle," he added, trying to reach it from the fork, where it hung high above Jacob's tall shoulder.

But Jacob showed as much alacrity in obeying as a wasp shows in leaving a sugar-basin. Near David, he felt himself in the vicinity of lozenges: he chuckled and rubbed his brother's back, brandishing the bundle higher out of reach. David, with an inward groan, changed his tactics, and walked on as fast as he could. It was not safe to linger. Jacob would get tired of following him, or, at all events, could be eluded. If they could once get to the distant highroad, a coach would overtake them, David would mount it, having previously by some ingenious means secured his bundle, and then Jacob might howl and flourish his pitchfork as much as he liked. Meanwhile he was under the fatal necessity of being very kind to this ogre, and of providing a large breakfast for him when they stopped at a roadside inn. It was already three hours since they had started, and David was tired. Would no coach be coming up soon? he inquired. No coach for the next two hours. But there was a carrier's cart to come immediately, on its way to the next town. If he could slip out, even leaving his bundle behind, and get into the cart without Jacob! But there was a new obstacle. Jacob had recently discovered a remnant of sugar-candy in one of his brother's tail-pockets; and, since then, had cautiously kept his hold on that limb of the garment, perhaps with an expectation that there would be a further development of sugar-candy after a longer or shorter interval. Now every one who has worn a coat will understand the sensibilities that must keep a man from starting away in a hurry when there is a grasp on his coat-tail. David looked forward to being well received among strangers, but it might make a difference if he had only one tail to his coat.

He felt himself in a cold perspiration. He could walk no more: he must get into the cart and let Jacob get in with him. Presently a cheering idea occurred to him: after so large a breakfast, Jacob would be sure to go to sleep in the cart; you see at once that David meant to seize his bundle, jump out, and be free. His expectation was partly fulfilled: Jacob did go to sleep in the cart, but it was in a peculiar attitude—it was with his arms tightly fastened round his dear brother's body; and if ever David attempted to move, the grasp tightened with the force of an affectionate boa-constrictor.

"Th' innicent's fond on you," observed the carrier, thinking that David was probably an amiable brother, and wishing to pay him a compliment.

David groaned. The ways of thieving were not ways of pleasantness. Oh, why had he an idiot brother? Oh, why, in general, was the world so constituted that a man could not take his mother's guineas comfortably? David became grimly speculative.

Copious dinner at noon for Jacob; but little dinner, because little appetite, for David. Instead of eating, he plied Jacob with beer; for through this liberality he descried a hope. Jacob fell into a dead sleep, at last, without having his arms round David, who paid the reckoning, took his bundle, and walked off. In another half-hour he was on the coach on his way to Liverpool, smiling the smile of the triumphant wicked. He was rid of Jacob—he was bound for the Indies, where a gullible princess awaited him. He would never steal any more, but there would be no need; he would show himself so deserving, that people would make him presents freely. He must give up the notion of his father's legacy; but it was not likely he would ever want that trifle; and even if he did—why, it was a compensation to think that in being for ever divided from his family he was divided from Jacob, more terrible than Gorgon or Demogorgon to David's timid green eyes. Thank heaven, he should never see Jacob any more!

2

IT WAS NEARLY six years after the departure of Mr. David Faux for the West Indies, that the vacant shop in the market-place at Grimworth was understood to have been let to the stranger with a sallow complexion and a buff cravat, whose first appearance had caused some excitement in the bar of the Woolpack, where he had called to wait for the coach.

Grimworth, to a discerning eye, was a good place to set up shopkeeping in. There was no competition in it at present; the Church-people had their own grocer and draper; the Dissenters had theirs; and the two or three butchers found a ready market for their joints without strict reference to religious persuasion—except that the rector's wife had given a general order for the veal sweet-breads and the mutton kidneys, while Mr. Rodd, the Baptist minister, had requested that, so far as was compatible with the fair accommodation of other customers, the sheep's trotters might be reserved for him. And it was likely to be a growing place, for the trustees of Mr. Zephaniah Crypt's Charity, under the stimulus of a late visitation by commissioners, were beginning to apply long-accumulating funds to the rebuilding of the Yellow Coat School, which was henceforth to be carried forward on a greatly-extended scale, the testator having left no restrictions concerning the curriculum, but only concerning the coat.

The shopkeepers at Grimworth were by no means unanimous as to the advantages promised by this prospect of increased population and trading, being substantial men, who liked doing a quiet business in which they were sure of their customers, and could calculate their returns to a nicety. Hitherto, it had been held a point of honour by the families in Grimworth parish, to buy their sugar and their flannel at the shop where their fathers and mothers had bought before them; but, if newcomers were to bring in the system of neck-and-neck trading, and solicit feminine eyes by gown-pieces laid in fan-like folds, and surmounted by artificial flowers, giving them a factitious charm (for on what human figure would a gown sit like a fan, or what female head was like a bunch of China-asters?), or, if new grocers were to fill their windows with mountains of currants and sugar, made seductive by contrast and tickets,—what security was there for Grimworth, that a vagrant spirit in shopping, once introduced, would not in the end carry the most important families to the larger market town of Cattleton, where, business being done on a system of small profits and quick returns, the fashions were of the freshest, and goods of all kinds might be bought at an advantage?

With this view of the times predominant among the tradespeople at Grimworth, their uncertainty concerning the nature of the business which the sallow-complexioned stranger was about to set up in the vacant shop, naturally gave some additional strength to the fears of the less sanguine. If he was going to sell drapery, it was probable that a pale-faced fellow like that would deal in showy and inferior articles—printed cottons and muslins which would leave their dye in the wash-tub, jobbed linen full of knots, and flannel that would soon look like gauze. If grocery, then it was to be hoped that no mother of a family would trust the teas of an untried grocer. Such things had been known in some parishes as tradesmen going about canvassing for custom with cards in their pockets: when people came from nobody knew where, there was no knowing what they might do. It was a thousand pities that Mr. Moffat, the auctioneer and broker, had died without leaving anybody to follow him in the business, and Mrs. Cleve's trustee ought to have known better than to let a shop to a stranger. Even the discovery that ovens were being put up on the premises, and that the shop was, in fact, being fitted up for a confectioner and pastry-cook's business, hitherto unknown in Grimworth, did not quite suffice to turn the scale in the newcomer's favour, though the landlady at the Woolpack defended him warmly, said he seemed to be a very clever young man, and from what she could make out, came of a very good family; indeed, was most likely a good many people's betters.

It certainly made a blaze of light and colour, almost as if a rainbow had suddenly descended into the market-place, when, one fine morning, the shutters were taken down from the new shop, and the two windows displayed their decorations. On one side, there were the variegated tints of collared and marbled meats, set off by bright green leaves, the pale brown of glazed pies, the rich tones of sauces and bottled fruits enclosed in their veil of glass—altogether a sight to bring tears into the eyes of a Dutch painter; and on the other, there was a predominance of the more delicate hues of pink, and white, and yellow, and buff, in the abundant lozenges, candies, sweet biscuits and icings, which to the eyes of a bilious person might easily have been blended into a faëry landscape in Turner's latest style. What a sight to dawn upon the eyes of Grimworth children! They almost forgot to go to their dinner that day, their appetites being preoccupied with imaginary sugar-plums; and I think even Punch, setting up his tabernacle in the market-place, would not have succeeded in drawing them away from those shop-windows, where they stood according to gradations of size and strength, the biggest and strongest being nearest the window, and the little ones in the outermost rows lifting wide-open eyes and mouths towards the upper tier of jars, like small birds at meal-time.

The elder inhabitants pished and pshawed a little at the folly of the new shopkeeper in venturing on such an outlay in goods that would not keep; to be sure, Christmas was coming, but what housewife in Grimworth would not think shame to furnish forth her table with articles that were not home-cooked? No, no. Mr. Edward Freely, as he called himself, was deceived, if he thought Grimworth money was to flow into his pockets on such terms.

Edward Freely was the name that shone in gilt letters on a mazarine ground over the doorplace of the new shop—a generous-sounding name, that might have belonged to the open-hearted, improvident hero of an old comedy, who would have delighted in raining sugared almonds, like a new manna-gift, among that small generation outside the windows. But Mr. Edward Freely was a man whose impulses were kept in due subordination: he held that the desire for sweets and pastry must only be satisfied in a direct ratio with the power of paying for them. If the smallest child in Grimworth would go to him with a halfpenny in its tiny fist, he would, after ringing the halfpenny, deliver a just equivalent in "rock." He was not a man to cheat even the smallest child—he often said so, observing at the same time that he loved honesty, and also that he was very tender-hearted, though he didn't show his feelings as some people did.

Either in reward of such virtue, or according to some more hidden law of sequence, Mr. Freely's business, in spite of prejudice, started under favourable auspices. For Mrs. Chaloner, the rector's wife, was among the earliest customers at the shop, thinking it only right to encourage a new parishioner who had made a decorous appearance at church; and she found Mr. Freely a most civil, obliging young man, and intelligent to a surprising degree for a confectioner; well-principled, too, for in giving her useful hints about choosing sugars he had thrown much light on the dishonesty of other tradesmen. Moreover, he had been in the West Indies, and had seen the very estate which had been her poor grandfather's property; and he said the missionaries were the only cause of the negro's discontent —an observing young man, evidently. Mrs. Chaloner ordered wine-biscuits and olives, and gave Mr. Freely to understand that she should find his shop a great convenience. So did the doctor's wife, and so did Mrs. Gate, at the large carding-mill, who, having high connexions frequently visiting her, might be expected to have a large consumption of ratafias and macaroons.

The less aristocratic matrons of Grimworth seemed likely at first to justify their husbands' confidence that they would never pay a percentage of profits on drop-cakes, instead of making their own, or get up a hollow show of liberal housekeeping by purchasing slices of collared meat when a neighbour came in for supper. But it is my task to narrate the gradual corruption of Grimworth manners from their primitive simplicity—a melancholy task, if it were not cheered by the prospect of the fine peripateia or downfall by which the progress of the corruption was ultimately checked.

It was young Mrs. Steene, the veterinary surgeon's wife, who first gave way to temptation. I fear she had been rather over-educated for her station in life, for she knew by heart many passages in *Lalla Rookh*, the *Corsair*, and the *Siege of Corinth*, which had given her a distaste for domestic occupations, and caused her a withering disappointment at the discovery that Mr. Steene, since his marriage, had lost all interest in the "bulbul," openly preferred discussing the nature of spavin with a coarse neighbour, and was angry if the pudding turned out watery—indeed, was simply a top-booted "vet.", who came in hungry at dinner-time; and not in the least like a nobleman turned Corsair out of pure scorn for his race, or like a renegade with a turban and crescent, unless it were in the irritability of his temper. And scorn is such a very different thing in top-boots!

This brutal man had invited a supper-party for Christmas eve, when he would expect to see mince-pies on the table. Mrs. Steene had prepared her mince-meat, and had devoted much butter, fine flour, and labour, to the making of a batch of pies in the morning; but they proved to be so very heavy when they came out of the oven, that she could only think with trembling of the moment when her husband should catch sight of them on the supper-table. He would storm at her, she was certain; and before all the company; and then she should never help crying: it was so dreadful to think she had come to that, after the bulbul and everything! Suddenly the thought darted through her mind that *this once* she might send for a dish of mince-pies from Freely's: she knew he had some. But what was to become of the eighteen heavy mince-pies? Oh, it was of no use thinking about that; it was very expensive—indeed, making mince-pies at all was a great expense, when they were not sure to turn out well: it would be much better to buy them ready-made. You paid a little more for them, but there was no risk of waste.

Such was the sophistry with which this misguided young woman—enough. Mrs. Steene sent for the mince-pies, and, I am grieved to add, garbled her household accounts in order to conceal the fact from her husband. This was the second step in a downward course, all owing to a young woman's being out of harmony with her circumstances, yearning after renegades and bulbuls, and being subject to claims from a veterinary surgeon fond of mince-pies. The third step was to harden herself by telling the fact of the bought mince-pies to her intimate friend Mrs. Mole, who had already guessed it, and who subsequently encouraged herself in buying a mould of jelly, instead of exerting her own skill, by the reflection that "other people" did the same sort of thing. The infection spread; soon there was a party or clique in Grimworth on the side of "buying at Freely's"; and many husbands, kept for some time in the dark on this point, innocently swallowed at two mouthfuls a tart on which they were paying a profit of a hundred per cent., and as innocently encouraged a fatal disingenuousness in the partners of their bosoms by praising the pastry. Others, more keen-sighted, winked at the too frequent presentation on washing-days, and at impromptu suppers, of superior spiced-beef, which flattered their palates more than the cold remnants they had formerly been contented with. Every housewife who had once "bought at Freely's" felt a secret joy when she detected a similar perversion in her neighbour's practice, and soon only two or three old-fashioned mistresses of families held out in the protest against the growing demoralization, saying to their neighbours who came to sup with them, "I can't offer you Freely's beef, or Freely's cheesecakes; everything in our house is home-made; I'm afraid you'll hardly have any appetite for our plain pastry." The doctor, whose cook was not satisfactory, the curate, who kept no cook, and the mining agent, who was a great *bon vivant*, even began to rely on Freely for the greater part of their dinner, when they wished to give an entertainment of some brilliancy. In short, the business of manufacturing the more fanciful viands was fast passing out of the hinds of maids and matrons in private families, and was becoming the work of a special commercial organ.

I am not ignorant that this sort of thing is called the inevitable course of civilization, division of labour, and so forth, and that the maids and matrons may be said to have had their hands set free from cookery to add to the wealth of society in some other way. Only it happened at Grimworth, which, to be sure, was a low place, that the maids and matrons could do nothing with their hands at all better than cooking: not even those who had always made heavy cakes and leathery pastry. And so it came to pass, that the progress of civilization at Grimworth was not otherwise apparent than in the impoverishment of men, the gossiping idleness of women, and the heightening prosperity of Mr. Edward Freely.

The Yellow Coat School was a double source of profit to the calculating confectioner; for he opened an eating-room for the superior workmen employed on the new school, and he accommodated the pupils at the old school by giving great attention to the fancy-sugar department. When I think of the sweet-tasted swans and other ingenious white shapes crunched by the small teeth of that rising generation, I am glad to remember that a certain amount of calcareous food has been held good for young creatures whose bones are not quite formed; for I have observed these delicacies to have an inorganic flavour which would have recommended them greatly to that young lady of the *Spectator's* acquaintance who habitually made her dessert on the stems of tobacco-pipes.

As for the confectioner himself, he made his way gradually into Grimworth homes, as his commodities did, in spite of some initial repugnance. Somehow or other, his reception as a guest seemed a thing that required justifying, like the purchasing of his pastry. In the first place, he was a stranger, and therefore open to suspicion; secondly, the confectionery business was so entirely new at Grimworth, that its place in the scale of rank had not been distinctly ascertained. There was no doubt about drapers and grocers, when they came of good old Grimworth families, like Mr. Luff and Mr. Prettyman: they visited with the Palfreys, who farmed their own land, played many a game at whist with the doctor, and condescended a little towards the timber-merchant, who had lately taken to the coal-trade also, and had got new furniture; but whether a confectioner should be admitted to this higher level of respectability, or should be understood to find his associates among butchers and bakers, was a new question on which tradition threw no light. His being a bachelor was in his favour, and would perhaps have been enough to turn the scale, even if Mr. Edward Freely's other personal pretensions had been of an entirely insignificant cast. But so far from this, it very soon appeared that he was a remarkable young man, who had been in the West Indies, and had seen many wonders by sea and land, so that he could charm the ears of Grimworth Desdemonas with stories of strange fishes, especially sharks, which he had stabbed in the nick of time by bravely plunging overboard just as the monster was turning on his side to devour the cook's mate; of terrible fevers which he had undergone in a land where the wind blows from all quarters at once; of rounds of toast cut straight from the breadfruit trees; of toes bitten off by land-crabs; of large honours that had been offered to him as a man who knew what was what, and was therefore particularly needed in a tropical climate; and of a Creole heiress who had wept bitterly at his departure. Such conversational talents as these, we know, will overcome disadvantages of complexion; and young Towers, whose cheeks were of the finest pink, set off by a fringe of dark whisker, was quite eclipsed by the presence of the sallow Mr. Freely. So exceptional a confectioner elevated the business, and might well begin to make disengaged hearts flutter a little.

Fathers and mothers were naturally more slow and cautious in their recognition of the newcomer's merits.

"He's an amusing fellow," said Mr. Prettyman, the highly respectable grocer. (Mrs. Prettyman was a Miss Fothergill, and her sister had married a London mercer.) "He's an amusing fellow; and I've no objection to his making one at the Oyster Club; but he's a bit too fond of riding the high horse. He's uncommonly knowing, I'll allow; but how came he to go to the Indies? I should like that answered. It's unnatural in a confectioner. I'm not fond of people that have been beyond seas, if they can't give a good account how they happened to go. When folks go so far off, it's because they've got little credit nearer home—that's my opinion. However, he's got some good rum; but I don't want to be hand and glove with him, for all that."

It was this kind of dim suspicion which beclouded the view of Mr. Freely's qualities in the maturer minds of Grimworth through the early months of his residence there. But when the confectioner ceased to be a novelty, the suspicions also ceased to be novel, and people got tired of hinting at them, especially as they seemed to be refuted by his advancing prosperity and importance. Mr. Freely was becoming a person of influence in the parish; he was found useful as an overseer of the poor, having great firmness in enduring other people's pain, which firmness, he said, was due to his great benevolence; he always did what was good for people in the end. Mr. Chaloner had even selected him as clergyman's churchwarden, for he was a very handy man, and much more of Mr. Chaloner's opinion in everything about church business than the older parishioners. Mr. Freely was a very regular churchman, but at the Oyster Club he was sometimes a little free in his conversation, more than hinting at a life of Sultanic self-indulgence which he had passed in the West Indies, shaking his head now and then and smiling rather bitterly, as men are wont to do when they intimate that they have become a little too wise to be instructed about a world which has long been flat and stale to them.

For some time he was quite general in his attentions to the fair sex, combining the gallantries of a lady's man with a severity of criticism on the person and manners of absent belles, which tended rather to stimulate in the feminine breast the desire to conquer the approval of so fastidious a judge. Nothing short of the very best in the department of female charms and virtues could suffice to kindle the ardour of Mr. Edward Freely, who had become familiar with the most luxuriant and dazzling beauty in the West Indies. It may seem incredible that a confectioner should have ideas and conversation so much resembling those to be met with in a higher walk of life, but it must be remembered that he had not merely travelled, he had also bow-legs and a sallow, small-featured visage, so that nature herself had stamped him for a fastidious connoisseur of the fair sex.

At last, however, it seemed clear that Cupid had found a sharper arrow than usual, and that Mr. Freely's heart was pierced. It was the general talk among the young people at Grimworth. But was it really love, and not rather ambition? Miss Fullilove, the timber-merchant's daughter, was quite sure that if *she* were Miss Penny Palfrey, she would be cautious; it was not a good sign when men looked so much above themselves for a wife. For it was no less a person than Miss Penelope Palfrey, second daughter of the Mr. Palfrey who farmed his own land, that had attracted Mr. Freely's peculiar regard, and conquered his fastidiousness; and no wonder, for the Ideal, as exhibited in the finest waxwork, was perhaps never so closely approached by the Real as in the person of the pretty Penelope. Her yellowish flaxen hair did not curl naturally, I admit, but its bright crisp ringlets were such smooth, perfect miniature tubes, that you would have longed to pass your little finger through them, and feel their soft elasticity. She wore them in a crop, for in those days, when society was in a healthier state, young ladies wore crops long after they were twenty, and Penelope was not yet nineteen. Like the waxen ideal, she had round blue eyes, and round nostrils in her little nose, and teeth such as the ideal would be seen to have, if it ever showed them. Altogether, she was a small, round thing, as neat as a pink and white double daisy, and as guileless; for I hope it does not argue guile in a pretty damsel of nineteen, to think that she should like to have a beau and be "engaged," when her elder sister had already been in that position a year and a half. To be sure, there was young Towers always coming to the house; but Penny felt convinced he only came to see her brother, for he never had anything to say to her, and never offered her his arm, and was as awkward and silent as possible.

It is not unlikely that Mr. Freely had early been smitten by Penny's charms, as brought under his observation at church, but he had to make his way in society a little before he could come into nearer contact with them; and even after he was well received in Grimworth families, it was a long while before he could converse with Penny otherwise than in an incidental meeting at Mr. Luff's. It was not so easy to get invited to Long Meadows, the residence of the Palfreys; for though Mr. Palfrey had been losing money of late years, not being able quite to recover his feet after the terrible murrain which forced him to borrow, his family were far from considering themselves on the same level even as the old-established tradespeople with whom they visited. The greatest people, even kings and queens, must visit with somebody, and the equals of the great are scarce. They were especially scarce at Grimworth, which, as I have before observed, was a low parish, mentioned with the most scornful brevity in gazetteers. Even the great people there were far behind those of their own standing in other parts of this realm. Mr. Palfrey's farmyard doors had the paint all worn off them, and the front garden walks had long been merged in a general weediness. Still, his father had been called Squire Palfrey, and had been respected by the last Grimworth generation as a man who could afford to drink too much in his own house.

Pretty Penny was not blind to the fact that Mr. Freely admired her, and she felt sure that it was he who had sent her a beautiful valentine; but her sister seemed to think so lightly of him (all young ladies think lightly of the gentlemen to whom they are not engaged), that Penny never dared mention him, and trembled and blushed whenever they met him, thinking of the valentine, which was very strong in its expressions, and which she felt guilty of knowing by heart. A man who had been to the Indies, and knew the sea so well, seemed to her a sort of public character, almost like Robinson Crusoe or Captain Cook; and Penny had always wished her husband to be a remarkable personage, likely to be put in Mangnall's Questions, with which register of the immortals she had become acquainted during her one year at a boarding-school. Only it seemed strange that a remarkable man should be a confectioner and pastry-cook, and this anomaly quite disturbed Penny's dreams. Her brothers, she knew, laughed at men who couldn't sit on horseback well, and called them tailors; but her brothers were very rough, and were quite without that power of anecdote which made Mr. Freely such a delightful companion. He was a very good man, she thought, for she had heard him say at Mr. Luff's, one day, that he always wished to do his duty in whatever state of life he might be placed; and he knew a great deal of poetry, for one day he had repeated a verse of a song. She wondered if he had made the words of the valentine!—it ended in this way:—

> "Without thee, it is pain to live,
> But with thee, it were sweet to die."

Poor Mr. Freely! her father would very likely object—she felt sure he would, for he always called Mr. Freely "that sugar-plum fellow." Oh, it was very cruel, when true love was crossed in that way, and all because Mr. Freely was a confectioner: well, Penny would be true to him, for all that, and since his being a confectioner gave her an opportunity of showing her faithfulness, she was glad of it. Edward Freely was a pretty name, much better than John Towers. Young Towers had offered her a rose out of his button-hole the other day, blushing very much; but she refused it, and thought with delight how much Mr. Freely would be comforted if he knew her firmness of mind.

Poor little Penny! the days were so very long among the daisies on a grazing farm, and thought is so active—how was it possible that the inward drama should not get the start of the outward? I have known young ladies, much better educated, and with an outward world diversified by instructive lectures, to say nothing of literature and highly-developed fancy-work, who have spun a cocoon of visionary joys and sorrows for themselves, just as Penny did. Her elder sister Letitia, who had a prouder style of beauty, and a more worldly ambition, was engaged to a wool-factor, who came all the way from Cattelton to see her; and everybody knows that a wool-factor takes a very high rank, sometimes driving a double-bodied gig. Letty's notions got higher every day, and Penny never dared to speak of her cherished griefs to her lofty sister—never dared to propose that they should call at Mr. Freely's to buy liquorice, though she had prepared for such an incident by mentioning a slight sore throat. So she had to pass the shop on the other side of the market-place, and reflect, with a suppressed sigh, that behind those pink and white jars somebody was thinking of her tenderly, unconscious of the small space that divided her from him.

And it was quite true that, when business permitted, Mr. Freely thought a great deal of Penny. He thought her prettiness comparable to the loveliest things in confectionery; he judged her to be of submissive temper—likely to wait upon him as well as if she had been a negress, and to be silently terrified when his liver made him irritable; and he considered the Palfrey family quite the best in the parish, possessing marriageable daughters. On the whole, he thought her worthy to become Mrs. Edward Freely, and all the more so, because it would probably require some ingenuity to win her. Mr. Palfrey was capable of horse-whipping a too rash pretender to his daughter's hand; and, moreover, he had three tall sons: it was clear that a suitor would be at a disadvantage with such a family, unless travel and natural acumen had given him a countervailing power of contrivance. And the first idea that occurred to him in the matter was, that Mr. Palfrey would object less if he knew that the Freelys were a much higher family than his own. It had been foolish modesty in him hitherto to conceal the fact that a branch of the Freelys held a manor in Yorkshire, and to shut up the portrait of his great uncle the admiral, instead of hanging it up where a family portrait should be hung—over the mantelpiece in the parlour. Admiral Freely, K.C.B., once placed in this conspicuous position, was seen to have had one arm only, and one eye—in these points resembling the heroic Nelson—while a certain pallid insignificance of feature confirmed the relationship between himself and his grand-nephew.

Next, Mr. Freely was seized with an irrepressible ambition to posses Mrs. Palfrey's receipt for brawn, hers being pronounced on all hands to be superior to his own—as he informed her in a very flattering letter carried by his errand-boy. Now Mrs. Palfrey, like other geniuses, wrought by instinct rather than by rule, and possessed no receipts—indeed, despised all people who used them, observing that people who pickled by book, must pickle by weights and measures, and such nonsense; as for herself, her weights and measures were the tip of her finger and the tip of her tongue, and if you went nearer, why, of course, for dry goods like flour and spice, you went by handfuls and pinches, and for wet, there was a middle-sized jug—quite the best thing whether for much or little, because you might know how much a teacupful was if you'd got any use of your senses, and you might be sure it would take five middle-sized jugs to make a gallon. Knowledge of this kind is like Titian's colouring, difficult to communicate; and as Mrs. Palfrey, once remarkably handsome, had now become rather stout and asthmatical, and scarcely ever left home, her oral teaching could hardly be given anywhere except at Long Meadows. Even a matron is not insusceptible to flattery, and the prospect of a visitor whose great object would be to listen to her conversation, was not without its charms to Mrs. Palfrey. Since there was no receipt to be sent in reply to Mr. Freely's humble request, she called on her more docile daughter, Penny, to write a note, telling him that her mother would be glad to see him and talk with him on brawn, any day that he could call at Long Meadows. Penny obeyed with a trembling hand, thinking how wonderfully things came about in this world.

In this way, Mr. Freely got himself introduced into the home of the Palfreys, and notwithstanding a tendency in the male part of the family to jeer at him a little as "peaky" and bow-legged, he presently established his position as an accepted and frequent guest. Young Towers looked at him with increasing disgust when they met at the house on a Sunday, and secretly longed to try his ferret upon him, as a piece of vermin which that valuable animal would be likely to tackle with unhesitating vigour. But—so blind sometimes are parents —neither Mr. nor Mrs. Palfrey suspected that Penny would have anything to say to a tradesman of questionable rank whose youthful bloom was much withered. Young Towers, they thought, had an eye to her, and *that* was likely enough to be a match some day; but Penny was a child at present. And all the while Penny was imagining the circumstances under which Mr. Freely would make her an offer: perhaps down by the row of damson-trees, when they were in the garden before tea; perhaps by letter—in which case, how would the letter begin? "Dearest Penelope?" or "My dear Miss Penelope?" or straight off, without dear anything, as seemed the most natural when people were embarrassed? But, however he might make the offer, she would not accept it without her father's consent: she would always be true to Mr. Freely, but she would not disobey her father. For Penny was a good girl, though some of her female friends were afterwards of opinion that it spoke ill for her not to have felt an instinctive repugnance to Mr. Freely.

But he was cautious, and wished to be quite sure of the ground he trod on. His views on marriage were not entirely sentimental, but were as duly mingled with considerations of what would be advantageous to a man in his position, as if he had had a very large amount of money spent on his education. He was not a man to fall in love in the wrong place; and so, he applied himself quite as much to conciliate the favour of the parents, as to secure the attachment of Penny. Mrs. Palfrey had not been inaccessible to flattery, and her husband, being also of mortal mould, would not, it might be hoped, be proof against rum—that very fine Jamaica rum—of which Mr. Freely expected always to have a supply sent him from Jamaica. It was not easy to get Mr. Palfrey into the parlour behind the shop, where a mild back-street light fell on the features of the heroic admiral; but by getting hold of him rather late one evening as he was about to return home from Grimworth, the aspiring lover succeeded in persuading him to sup on some collared beef which, after Mrs. Palfrey's brawn, he would find the very best of cold eating.

From that hour Mr. Freely felt sure of success: being in privacy with an estimable man old enough to be his father, and being rather lonely in the world, it was natural he should unbosom himself a little on subjects which he could not speak of in a mixed circle—especially concerning his expectations from his uncle in Jamaica, who had no children, and loved his nephew Edward better than any one else in the world, though he had been so hurt at his leaving Jamaica, that he had threatened to cut him off with a shilling. However, he had since written to state his full forgiveness, and though he was an eccentric old gentleman and could not bear to give away money during his life, Mr. Edward Freely could show Mr. Palfrey the letter which declared, plainly enough, who would be the affectionate uncle's heir. Mr. Palfrey actually saw the letter, and could not help admiring the spirit of the nephew who declared that such brilliant hopes as these made no difference to his conduct; he should work at his humble business and make his modest fortune at it all the same. If the Jamaica estate was to come to him—well and good. It was nothing very surprising for one of the Freely family to have an estate left him, considering the lands that family had possessed in time gone by—nay, still possessed in the Northumberland branch. Would not Mr. Palfrey take another glass of rum? and also look at the last year's balance of the accounts? Mr. Freely was a man who cared to possess personal virtues, and did not pique himself on his family, though some men would.

We know how easily the great Leviathan may be led, when once there is a hook in his nose or a bridle in his jaws. Mr. Palfrey was a large man, but, like Leviathan's, his bulk went against him when once he had taken a turning. He was not a mercurial man, who easily changed his point of view. Enough. Before two months were over, he had given his consent to Mr. Freely's marriage with his daughter Penny, and having hit on a formula by which he could justify it, fenced off all doubts and objections, his own included. The formula was this: "I'm not a man to put my head up an entry before I know where it leads."

Little Penny was very proud and fluttering, but hardly so happy as she expected to be in an engagement. She wondered if young Towers cared much about it, for he had not been to the house lately, and her sister and brothers were rather inclined to sneer than to sympathize. Grimworth rang with the news. All men extolled Mr. Freely's good fortune; while the women, with the tender solicitude characteristic of the sex, wished the marriage might turn out well.

While affairs were at this triumphant juncture, Mr. Freely one morning observed that a stone-carver who had been breakfasting in the eating-room had left a newspaper behind. It was the *X-shire Gazette,* and X-shire being a county not unknown to Mr. Freely, he felt some curiosity to glance over it, and especially over the advertisements. A slight flush came over his face as he read. It was produced by the following announcement:—"If David Faux, son of Jonathan Faux, late of Gilsbrook, will apply at the office of Mr. Strutt, attorney, of Rodham, he will hear of something to his advantage."

"Father's dead!" exclaimed Mr. Freely, involuntarily. "Can he have left me a legacy?"

3

Perhaps it was a result quite different from your expectations, that Mr. David Faux should have returned from the West Indies only a few years after his arrival there, and have set up in his old business, like any plain man who has never travelled. But these cases do occur in life. Since, as we know, men change their skies and see new constellations without changing their souls, it will follow sometimes that they don't change their business under those novel circumstances.

Certainly, this result was contrary to David's own expectations. He had looked forward, you are aware, to a brilliant career among "the blacks"; but, either because they had already seen too many white men, or for some other reason, they did not at once recognize him as a superior order of human being; besides, there were no princesses among them. Nobody in Jamaica was anxious to maintain David for the mere pleasure of his society; and those hidden merits of a man which are so well known to himself were as little recognized there as they notoriously are in the effete society of the Old World. So that in the dark hints that David threw out at the

Oyster Club about that life of Sultanic self-indulgence spent by him in the luxurious Indies, I really think he was doing himself a wrong; I believe he worked for his bread, and, in fact, took to cooking as, after all, the only department in which he could offer skilled labour. He had formed several ingenious plans by which he meant to circumvent people of large fortune and small faculty; but then he never met with exactly the right circumstances. David's devices for getting rich without work had apparently no direct relation with the world outside him, as his confectionery receipts had. It is possible to pass a great many bad half pennies and bad half-crowns, but I believe there has no instance been known of passing a halfpenny or a half-crown as a sovereign. A sharper can drive a brisk trade in this world: it is undeniable that there may be a fine career for him, if he will dare consequences; but David was too timid to be a sharper, or venture in any way among the mantraps of the law. He dared rob nobody but his mother. And so he had to fall back on the genuine value there was in him—to be content to pass as a good halfpenny, or, to speak more accurately, as a good confectioner. For in spite of some additional reading and observation, there was nothing else he could make so much money by; nay, he found in himself even a capability of extending his skill in this direction, and embracing all forms of cookery; while, in other branches of human labour, he began to see that it was not possible for him to shine. Fate was too strong for him; he had thought to master her inclination and had fled over the seas to that end; but she caught him, tied an apron round him, and snatching him from all other devices, made him devise cakes and patties in a kitchen at Kingstown. He was getting submissive to her, since she paid him with tolerable gains; but fevers and prickly heat, and other evils incidental to cooks in ardent climates, made him long for his native land; so he took ship once more, carrying his six years' savings, and seeing distinctly, this time, what were Fate's intentions as to his career. If you question me closely as to whether all the money with which he set up at Grimworth consisted of pure and simple earnings, I am obliged to confess that he got a sum or two for charitably abstaining from mentioning some other people's misdemeanours. Altogether, since no prospects were attached to his family name, and since a new christening seemed a suitable commencement of a new life, Mr. David Faux thought it as well to call himself Mr. Edward Freely.

But lo! now, in opposition to all calculable probability, some benefit appeared to be attached to the name of David Faux. Should he neglect it, as beneath the attention of a prosperous tradesman? It might bring him into contact with his family again, and he felt no yearnings in that direction: moreover, he had small belief that the "something to his advantage" could be anything considerable. On the other hand, even a small gain is pleasant, and the promise of it in this instance was so surprising, that David felt his curiosity awakened. The scale dipped at last on the side of writing to the lawyer, and, to be brief, the correspondence ended in an appointment for a meeting between David and his eldest brother at Mr. Strutt's, the vague "something" having been defined as a legacy from his father of eighty-two pounds, three shillings.

David, you know, had expected to be disinherited; and so he would have been, if he had not, like some other indifferent sons, come of excellent parents, whose conscience made them scrupulous where much more highly-instructed people often feel themselves warranted in following the bent of their indignation. Good Mrs. Faux could never forget that she had brought this ill-conditioned son into the world when he was in that entirely helpless state which excluded the smallest choice on his part; and, somehow or other, she felt that his going wrong would be his father's and mother's fault, if they failed in one tittle of their parental duty. Her notion of parental duty was not of a high and subtle kind, but it included giving him his due share of the family property; for when a man had got a little honest money of his own, was he so likely to steal? To cut the delinquent son off with a shilling, was like delivering him over to his evil propensities. No; let the sum of twenty guineas which he had stolen be deducted from his share, and then let the sum of three guineas be put back from it, seeing that his mother had always considered three of the twenty guineas as his; and, though he had run away, and was, perhaps, gone across the sea, let the money be left to him all the same, and be kept in reserve for his possible return. Mr. Faux agreed to his wife's views, and made a codicil to his will accordingly, in time to die with a clear conscience. But for some time his family thought it likely that David would never reappear; and the eldest son, who had the charge of Jacob on his hands, often thought it a little hard that David might perhaps be dead, and yet, for want of certitude on that point, his legacy could not fall to his legal heir. But in this state of things the opposite certitude—namely, that David was still alive and in England—seemed to be brought by the testimony of a neighbour, who, having been on a journey to Cattelton, was pretty sure he had seen David in a gig, with a stout man driving by his side. He could "swear it was David," though he could "give no account why, for he had no marks on him; but no more had a white dog, and that didn't hinder folks from knowing a white dog." It was this incident which had led to the advertisement.

The legacy was paid, of course, after a few preliminary disclosures as to Mr. David's actual position. He begged to send his love to his mother, and to say that he hoped to pay her a dutiful visit by and by; but, at present, his business and near prospect of marriage made it difficult for him to leave home. His brother replied with much frankness.

"My mother may do as she likes about having you to see her, but, for my part, I don't want to catch sight of you on the premises again. When folks have taken a new name, they'd better keep to their new 'quinetance."

David pocketed the insult along with the eighty-two pounds three, and travelled home again in some triumph at the ease of a transaction which had enriched him to this extent. He had no intention of offending his brother by further claims on his fraternal recognition, and relapsed with full contentment into the character of Mr. Edward Freely, the orphan, scion of a great but reduced family, with an eccentric uncle in the West Indies. (I have already hinted that he had some acquaintance with imaginative literature; and being of a practical turn, he had, you perceive, applied even this form of knowledge to practical purposes.)

It was little more than a week after the return from his fruitful journey, that the day of his marriage with Penny having been fixed, it was agreed that Mrs. Palfrey should overcome her reluctance to move from home, and that she and her husband should bring their two daughters to inspect little Penny's future abode and decide on the new arrangements to be made for the reception of the bride. Mr. Freely meant her to have a house so pretty and comfortable that she need not envy even a wool-factor's wife. Of course, the upper room over the shop was to be the best sitting-room; but also the parlour behind the shop was to be made a suitable bower for the lovely Penny, who would naturally wish to be near her husband, though Mr. Freely declared his resolution never to allow *his* wife to wait in the shop. The decisions about the parlour furniture were left till last, because the party was to take tea there; and, about five o'clock, they were all seated there with the best muffins and buttered buns before them, little Penny blushing and smiling, with her "crop" in the best order, and a blue frock showing her little white shoulders, while her opinion was being always asked and never given. She secretly wished to have a particular sort of chimney ornaments, but she could not have brought herself to mention it. Seated by the side of her yellow and rather withered lover, who, though he had not reached his thirtieth year, had already crow's-feet about his eyes, she was quite tremulous at the greatness of her lot in being married to a man who had travelled so much—and before her sister Letty! The handsome Letitia looked rather proud and contemptuous, thought her nature brother-in-law an odious person, and was vexed with her father and mother for letting Penny marry him. Dear little Penny! She certainly did look like a fresh white-heart cherry going to be bitten off the stem by that lipless mouth. Would no deliverer come to make a slip between that cherry and that mouth without a lip?

"Quite a family likeness between the admiral and you, Mr. Freely," observed Mrs. Palfrey, who was looking at the family portrait for the first time. "It's wonderful! and only a grand-uncle. Do you feature the rest of your family, as you know of?"

"I can't say," said Mr. Freely, with a sigh. "My family have mostly thought themselves too high to take any notice of me."

At this moment an extraordinary disturbance was heard in the shop, as of a heavy animal stamping about and making angry noises, and then of a glass vessel falling in shivers, while the voice of the apprentice was heard calling "Master" in great alarm.

Mr. Freely rose in anxious astonishment, and hastened into the shop, followed by the four Palfreys, who made a group at the parlour-door, transfixed with wonder at seeing a large man in a smock-frock, with a pitchfork in his hand, rush up to Mr. Freely and hug him, crying out,—"Zavy, Zavy, b'other Zavy!"

It was Jacob, and for some moments David lost all presence of mind. He felt arrested for having stolen his mother's guineas. He turned cold, and trembled in his brother's grasp.

"Why, how's this?" said Mr. Palfrey, advancing from the door. "Who is he?"

Jacob supplied the answer by saying over and over again—

"I'se Zacob, b'other Zacob. Come 'o zee Zavy"—till hunger prompted him to relax his grasp, and to seize a large raised pie, which he lifted to his mouth.

By this time David's power of device had begun to return, but it was a very hard task for his prudence to master his rage and hatred towards poor Jacob.

"I don't know who he is; he must be drunk," he said, in a low tone to Mr. Palfrey. "But he's dangerous with that pitchfork. He'll never let it go." Then checking himself on the point of betraying too great an intimacy with Jacob's habits, he added "You watch him, while I run for the constable." And he hurried out of the shop.

"Why, where do you come from, my man?" said Mr. Palfrey, speaking to Jacob in a conciliatory tone. Jacob was eating his pie by large mouthfuls, and looking round at the other good things in the shop, while he embraced his pitchfork with his left arm, and laid his left hand on some Bath buns. He was in the rare position of a person who recovers a long absent friend and finds him richer than ever in the characteristics that won his heart.

"I's Zacob—b'other Zacob—'t home. I love Zavy—b'other Zavy," he said, as soon as Mr. Palfrey had drawn his attention. "Zavy come back from z' Indies—got mother's zinnies. Where's Zavy?" he added, looking round and then turning to the others with a questioning air, puzzled by David's disappearance.

"It's very odd," observed Mr. Palfrey to his wife and daughters. "He seems to say Freely's his brother come back from th' Indies."

"What a pleasant relation for us!" said Letitia, sarcastically. "I think he's a good deal like Mr. Freely. He's got just the same sort of nose, and his eyes are the same colour."

Poor Penny was ready to cry.

But now Mr. Freely re-entered the shop without the constable. During his walk of a few yards he had had time and calmness enough to widen his view of consequences, and he saw that to get Jacob taken to the workhouse or to the lock-up house as an offensive stranger might have awkward effects if his family took the trouble of inquiring after him. He must resign himself to more patient measures.

"On second thoughts," he said, beckoning to Mr. Palfrey and whispering to him while Jacob's back was turned, "he's a poor half-witted fellow. Perhaps his friends will come after him. I don't mind giving him something to eat, and letting him lie down for the night. He's got it into his head that he knows me—they do get these fancies, idiots do. He'll perhaps go away again in an hour or two, and make no more ado. I'm a kind-hearted man *myself*—I shouldn't like to have the poor fellow ill-used."

"Why, he'll eat a sovereign's worth in no time," said Mr. Palfrey, thinking Mr. Freely a little too magnificent in his generosity.

"Eh, Zavy, come back?" exclaimed Jacob, giving his dear brother another hug, which crushed Mr. Freely's features inconveniently against the stale of the pitchfork.

"Aye, aye," said Mr. Freely, smiling, with every capability of murder in his mind, except the courage to commit it. He wished the Bath buns might by chance have arsenic in them.

"Mother's zinnies?" said Jacob, pointing to a glass jar of yellow lozenges that stood in the window. "Zive 'em me."

David dared not do otherwise than reach down the glass jar and give Jacob a handful. He received them in his smock-frock, which he held out for more.

"They'll keep him quiet a bit, at any rate," thought David, and emptied the jar. Jacob grinned and mowed with delight.

"You're very good to this stranger, Mr. Freely," said Letitia; and then spitefully, as David joined the party at the parlour-door, "I think you could hardly treat him better, if he was really your brother."

"I've always thought it a duty to be good to idiots," said Mr. Freely, striving after the most moral view of the subject. "We might have been idiots ourselves—everybody might have been born idiots, instead of having their right senses."

"I don't know where there'd ha' been victual for us all then," observed Mrs. Palfrey, regarding the matter in a housewifely light.

"But let us sit down again and finish our tea," said Mr. Freely. "Let us leave the poor creature to himself."

They walked into the parlour again; but Jacob, not apparently appreciating the kindness of leaving him to himself, immediately followed his brother, and seated himself, pitchfork grounded, at the table.

"Well," said Miss Letitia, rising, "I don't know whether *you* mean to stay, mother; but I shall go home."

"Oh, me too," said Penny, frightened to death at Jacob, who had begun to nod and grin at her.

"Well, I think we *had* better be going, Mr. Palfrey," said the mother, rising more slowly.

Mr. Freely, whose complexion had become decidedly yellower during the last half-hour, did not resist this proposition. He hoped they should meet again "under happier circumstances."

"It's my belief the man is his brother," said Letitia, when they were all on their way home.

"Nonsense!" said Mr. Palfrey. "Freely's got no brother—he's said so many and many a time; he's an orphan; he's got nothing but uncles—leastwise, one. What's it matter what an idiot says? What call had Freely to tell lies?"

Letitia tossed her head and was silent.

Mr. Freely, left alone with his affectionate brother Jacob, brooded over the possibility of luring him out of the town early the next morning, and getting him conveyed to Gilsbrook without further betrayals. But the thing was difficult. He saw clearly that if he took Jacob himself, his absence, conjoined with the disappearance of the stranger, would either cause the conviction that he was really a relative, or would oblige him to the dangerous course of inventing a story to account for his disappearance, and his own absence at the same time. David groaned. There come occasions when falsehood is felt to be inconvenient. It would, perhaps, have been a longer-headed device, if he had never told any of those clever fibs about his uncles, grand and otherwise; for the Palfreys were simple people, and shared the popular prejudice against lying. Even if he could get Jacob away this time, what security was there that he would not come again, having once found the way? O guineas! O lozenges! what enviable people those were who had never robbed their mothers, and had never told fibs! David spent a sleepless night, while Jacob was snoring close by. Was this the upshot of travelling to the Indies, and acquiring experience combined with anecdote?

He rose at break of day, as he had once before done when he was in fear of Jacob, and took all gentle means to rouse this fatal brother from his deep sleep; he dared not be loud, because his apprentice was in the house, and would report everything. But Jacob was not to be roused. He fought out with his fist at the unknown cause of disturbance, turned over, and snored again. He must be left to wake as he would. David, with a cold perspiration on his brow, confessed to himself that Jacob could not be got away that day.

Mr. Palfrey came over to Grimworth before noon, with a natural curiosity to see how his future son-in-law got on with the stranger to whom he was so benevolently inclined. He found a crowd round the shop. All Grimworth by this time had heard how Freely had been fastened on by an idiot, who called him "Brother Zavy"; and the younger population seemed to find the singular stranger an unwearying source of fascination, while the householders dropped in one by one to inquire into the incident.

"Why don't you send him to the workhouse?" said Mr. Prettyman. "You'll have a row with him and the children presently, and he'll eat you up. The workhouse is the proper place for him; let his kin claim him, if he's got any."

"Those may be *your* feelings, Mr. Prettyman," said David, his mind quite enfeebled by the torture of his position.

"What! *is* he your brother, then?" said Mr. Prettyman, looking at his neighbour Freely rather sharply.

"All men are our brothers, and idiots particular so," said Mr. Freely, who, like many other travelled men, was not master of the English language.

"Come, come, if he's your brother, tell the truth, man," said Mr. Prettyman, with growing suspicion. "Don't be ashamed of your own flesh and blood."

Mr. Palfrey was present, and also had his eye on Freely. It is difficult for a man to believe in the advantage of a truth which will disclose him to have been a liar. In this critical moment, David shrank from this immediate disgrace in the eyes of his future father-in-law.

"Mr. Prettyman," he said, "I take your observations as an insult. I've no reason to be otherwise than proud of my own flesh and blood. If this poor man was my brother more than all men are, I should say so."

A tall figure darkened the door, and David, lifting his eyes in that direction, saw his eldest brother, Jonathan, on the door-sill.

"I'll stay wi' Zavy," shouted Jacob, as he, too, caught sight of his eldest brother; and, running behind the counter, he clutched David hard.

"What, he *is* here?" said Jonathan Faux, coming forward. "My mother would have no nay, as he'd been away so long, but I must see after him. And it struck me he was very like come after you, because we'd been talking of you o' late, and where you lived."

David saw there was no escape; he smiled a ghastly smile.

"What! is this a relation of yours, sir?" said Mr. Palfrey to Jonathan.

"Aye, it's my innicent of a brother, sure enough," said honest

Jonathan. "A fine trouble and cost he is to us, in th' eating and other things, but we must bear what's laid on us."

"And your name's Freely, is it?" said Mr. Prettyman.

"Nay, nay, my name's Faux, I know nothing o' Freelys," said Jonathan, curtly. "Come," he added, turning to David, "I must take some news to mother about Jacob. Shall I take him with me, or will you undertake to send him back?"

"Take him, if you can make him loose his hold of me," said David, feebly.

"Is this gentleman here in the confectionery line your brother, then, sir?" said Mr. Prettyman, feeling that it was an occasion on which formal language must be used.

"*I* don't want to own him," said Jonathan, unable to resist a movement of indignation that had never been allowed to satisfy itself. "He ran away from home with good reasons in his pocket years ago: he didn't want to be owned again, I reckon."

Mr. Palfrey left the shop; he felt his own pride too severely wounded by the sense that he had let himself be fooled, to feel curiosity for further details. The most pressing business was to go home and tell his daughter that Freely was a poor sneak, probably a rascal, and that her engagement was broken off.

Mr. Prettyman stayed, with some internal self-gratulation that *he* had never given in to Freely, and that Mr. Chaloner would see now what sort of fellow it was that he had put over the heads of older parishioners. He considered it due from him (Mr. Prettyman) that, for the interests of the parish, he should know all that was to be known about this "interloper." Grimworth would have people coming from Botany Bay to settle in it, if things went on in this way.

It soon appeared that Jacob could not be made to quit his dear brother David except by force. He understood, with a clearness equal to that of the most intelligent mind, that Jonathan would take him back to skimmed milk, apple-dumpling, broad beans, and pork.

And he had found a paradise in his brother's shop. It was a difficult matter to use force with Jacob, for he wore heavy nailed boots; and if his pitchfork had been mastered, he would have resorted without hesitation to kicks. Nothing short of using guile to bind him hand and foot would have made all parties safe.

"Let him stay," said David, with desperate resignation, frightened above all things at the idea of further disturbances in his shop, which would make his exposure all the more conspicuous. "*You* go away again, and to-morrow I can, perhaps, get him to go to Gilsbrook with me. He'll follow me fast enough, I daresay," he added, with a half-groan.

"Very well," said Jonathan, gruffly. "I don't see why *you* shouldn't have some trouble and expense with him as well as the rest of us. But mind you bring him back safe and soon, else mother'll never rest."

On this arrangement being concluded, Mr. Prettyman begged Mr. Jonathan Faux to go and take a snack with him, an invitation which was quite acceptable; and as honest Jonathan had nothing to be ashamed of, it is probable that he was very frank in his communications to the civil draper, who, pursuing the benefit of the parish, hastened to make all the information he could gather about Freely common parochial property. You may imagine that the meeting of the Club at the Woolpack that evening was unusually lively. Every member was anxious to prove that he had never liked Freely, as he called himself. Faux was his name, was it? Fox would have been more suitable. The majority expressed a desire to see him hooted out of the town.

Mr. Freely did not venture over his door-sill that day, for he knew Jacob would keep at his side, and there was every probability that they would have a train of juvenile followers. He sent to engage the Woolpack gig for an early hour the next morning; but this order was not kept religiously a secret by the landlord. Mr. Freely was informed that he could not have the gig till seven; and the Grimworth people were early risers. Perhaps they were more alert than usual on this particular morning; for when Jacob, with a bag of sweets in his hand, was induced to mount the gig with his brother David, the inhabitants of the market-place were looking out of their doors and windows, and at the turning of the street there was even a muster of apprentices and schoolboys, who shouted as they passed in what Jacob took to be a very merry and friendly way, nodding and grinning in return. "Huzzay, David Faux! how's your uncle?" was their morning's greeting. Like other pointed things, it was not altogether impromptu.

Even this public derision was not so crushing to David as the horrible thought that though he might succeed now in getting Jacob home again there would never be any security against his coming back, like a wasp to the honey-pot. As long as David lived at Grimworth, Jacob's return would be hanging over him. But could he go on living at Grimworth—an object of ridicule, discarded by the Palfreys, after having revelled in the consciousness that he was an envied and prosperous confectioner? David liked to be envied; he minded less about being loved.

His doubts on this point were soon settled. The mind of Grimworth became obstinately set against him and his viands, and the new school being finished, the eating-room was closed. If there had been no other reason, sympathy with the Palfreys, that respectable family who had lived in the parish time out of mind, would have determined all well-to-do people to decline Freely's goods. Besides, he had absconded with his mother's guineas: who knew what else he had done, in Jamaica or elsewhere, before he came to Grimworth, worming himself into families under false pretences? Females shuddered. Dreadful suspicions gathered round him: his green eyes, his bow-legs had a criminal aspect. The rector disliked the sight of a man who had imposed upon him; and all boys who could not afford to purchase, hooted "David Faux" as they passed his shop. Certainly no man now would pay anything for the "goodwill" of Mr. Freely's business, and he would be obliged to quit it without a peculium so desirable towards defraying the expense of moving.

In a few months the shop in the market-place was again to let, and Mr. David Faux, alias Mr. Edward Freely, had gone—nobody at Grimworth knew whither. In this way the demoralization of Grimworth women was checked. Young Mrs. Steene renewed her efforts to make light mince-pies, and having at last made a batch so excellent that Mr. Steene looked at her with complacency as he ate them, and said they were the best he had ever eaten in his life, she thought less of bulbuls and renegades ever after. The secrets of the finer cookery were revived in the breasts of matronly house-wives, and daughters were again anxious to be initiated in them.

You will further, I hope, be glad to hear, that some purchases of drapery made by pretty Penny, in preparation for her marriage with Mr. Freely, came in quite as well for her wedding with young Towers as if they had been made expressly for the latter occasion. For Penny's complexion had not altered, and blue always became it best.

Here ends the story of Mr. David Faux, confectioner, and his brother Jacob. And we see in it, I think, an admirable instance of the unexpected forms in which the great Nemesis hides herself.

Printed in Great Britain
by Amazon